Praise for Christopher Carmona's

EL RINCHE
The Ghost Ranger of the Rio Grande
Vol. 1

"A thrilling border saga ripped from the pages of Texas history, El Rinche: The Ghost Ranger of the Rio Grande, gives younger readers a crucial history lesson while keeping them turning pages! I only wish Carmona's novel had been around when I was a young reader. I'd have been wiser in understanding the experience of our people regarding "official" narratives that most often serve to whitewash Texas history. Best of all, it's a great read!"

—Manuel Luis Martinez, author of *Los Duros*, a novel and winner of the American Book Award

"A heart-pounding, powerful story about the undying spirit of the Plata family—and how they fight to defend their land from being stolen, even in death."

—Natalia Sylvester, author of Author of *Chasing The Sun* & *Everyone Knows You Go Home*

"A romping picaresque that insists on crossing borders—not just the physical one between Mexico and the United States, but the social borders between races and the lines between good and evil."

—Benjamin H. Johnson, author of *Revolution in Texas: How a Forgotten Rebellion and Its Bloody Suppression Turned Mexicans into Americans*

EL RINCHE

The Ghost Ranger of the Rio Grande

Vol. 1

CHRISTOPHER CARMONA

Jade
Publishing

.

Jade Publishing
Lubbock, TX 79410
www.jadepublishing.org
ISBN: 978-1-949299-03-8

Printed in the United States of America

Dedication

This book is dedicated to my grandfather, Jose Carmona [September 15, 1917 - May 20, 2012] who experienced, first-hand, the terror of the Texas Rangers. It was through the stories he used to tell me as a child that this story first had its seeds buried deep inside me. This book is also dedicated to all of the gente that experienced the brutality of the Texas Rangers and the criminal actions perpetrated by "American" expansionists that conspired to steal the land and rights of Mexican Tejanos during the time known as "The Troubles." Finally, this book is dedicated to the young kid who needs a hero in the darkest of moments. There is always hope even in a time when everything seems lost, and sometimes it comes in a mask with ninja skills.

Acknowledgments

I would like to acknowledge the people that helped me in the process of writing this book. First, I would like to thank Griselda Castillo for being a prudent reader of this book and for lending me her critical eye to help me shape this book to what it is now. I would like to thank Juan Ochoa and Oscar Garza III for writing the corrido for El Rinche. I would also like to thank Jiovanna Perez, for helping me coordinate the costume design for El Rinche, as well as helping me coordinate the vision of the characters of this book and for the artwork of this book. I would also like to thank Luis Corpus for doing an amazing job with the cover art. I would be remiss not to thank Juan Flores, Jr., who helped me navigate the Texas Ranger Commission Report and the various testimonies of the victims of the Ranger violence. Most importantly I would to thank the various people that helped me along the way with the research for the historical time period that El Rinche takes place such as my brother, Juan Carmona, and the scholars of the Refusing to Forget Project: Trinidad Gonzales, Sonia Hernandez, Juan Moran Gonzalez, Ben Johnson, and Monica Muñoz Martinez. [The Refusing to Forget project's work is extremely important in documenting the atrocities against Mexicanos and Mexican Americans during the era known as the Matanza 1910-1920. Please visit their website at www.refusingtoforget.org.] I would like to also acknowledge Linn Manuel Miranda who's play *Hamilton* taught me that I can tell this story in my own voice, even if that story challenges what we think we know about history. Finally, I want to acknowledge James

Baldwin, whose writings have deeply influenced me and my work. There is no other passage of Baldwin's writing that has influenced my writing of this book as this from *I Am Not Your Negro*: "It comes as a great shock…to discover that the flag to which you have pledged allegiance…has not pledged allegiance to you. It comes as a great shock to see Gary Cooper killing off the Indians, and although you are rooting for Gary Cooper, that the Indians are you."

EL RINCHE

The Ghost Ranger of the Rio Grande

Vol. 1

PART I

PART II

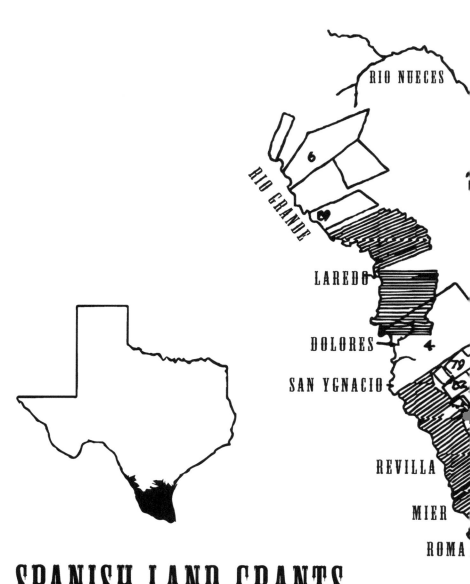

RIO NUECES

RIO GRANDE

6

LAREDO

DOLORES

SAN YGNACIO

4

REVILLA

MIER

ROMA

SPANISH LAND GRANTS
IN SOUTH TEXAS

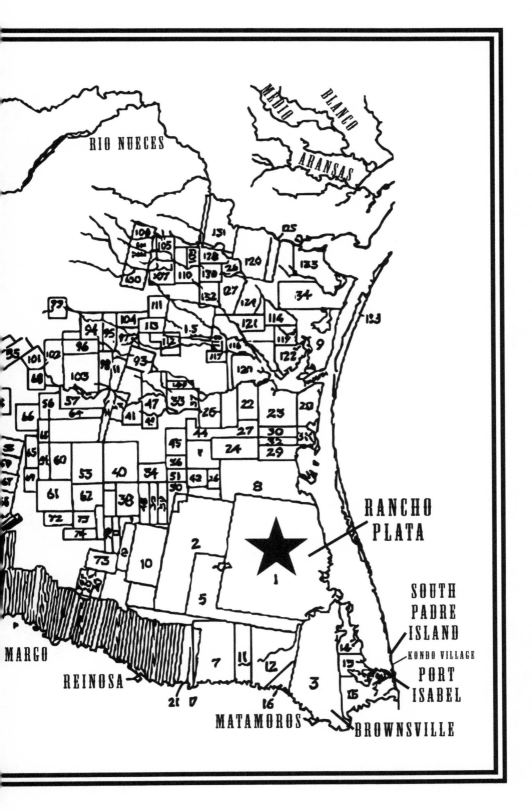

PART I

THOSE EYES

It all started with those eyes. *Esos ojos verdes.* They were the first thing that most people noticed about Ascensión Ruiz de Plata, or just Chonnie to everyone that knew him. Those eyes were so piercing that his mother, Herlinda, swore she could always find him in the dark. They were a beacon on nights when all you could see were miles of stars blanketing the world. She could always see his eyes. Curious, bright, and oh so much like hers. Of the two sons she had, he was the only one with her eyes. Chonnie was her little güerito. His father, Daniel, would sometimes call him Blondie because his hair was almost blonde. His brother, Macario would only call him Bolillo and never Chonnie. He hated being called Bolillo but Macario was older and bigger and better at everything.

Macario was tall, dark as coffee, and always good with horses, girls, and his fists. When he spoke, everyone listened. Daniel would always joke that Macario was born a man. He was never a boy. Chonnie, though, was good at reading, running away from Macario's golpes, and for a reason he never understood, he was a natural pistol shot. He preferred the Colt .45, but he could shoot well with any pistol. That was the only thing that he could do better than Macario that didn't involve books. Macario would never shoot pistols with Chonnie. He was too busy being Papá's favorite son. Macario was to run the rancho when Papá was gone.

The Plata Rancho sat just north of Brownsville. On the frontera between what used to be Mexico and what still is. The rancho was once a five-million-acre rancho granted to the Plata many years ago by a Spanish king from across the sea. But now it was only a few hundred acres, dwindled down by American progress and Anglo squatters. Anglo progress was a slow steamroll that inched closer and closer. And as the railroad came closer and closer, Mexican Tejanos like the Platas felt that the end of the 19th century brought the end of their way of life. Macario was supposed to be the great protector of the Plata Rancho. Everything depended on Macario, and Chonnie knew it.

So, Chonnie buried himself in books and spent much of his time alone and quiet. Daniel never paid much attention to him. Chonnie was Herlinda's boy. And Daniel never let Chonnie forget that. Even when he tried to join in and help with the vaqueroing, Daniel would just yell at him, "Entra a la casa y ayuda a tu madre."

"Pero Papá, I want to help."

"¡Ve ahora!"

And Chonnie would go. Deflated and defeated.

That all changed on February 20, 1890. It was Macario's sixteenth birthday and Daniel had gone all out. There were mariachis, a piñata for the kids, and even músicos for when the night got too late for the güercos. The fiesta was held in the courtyard of the hacienda where all the parties happened. The Platas employed several families on their rancho, but those kids never really liked Chonnie. He was too weird for them. So, Chonnie would often hide in places no one would look. That night promised to be no different, so he prepared to spend the day reading. But then, something happened. He saw something extraordinary. He saw them. *Otros ojos verdes*. But more importantly, he saw her.

The baile had kicked up. The clouds were so stubborn that day, they wouldn't let the sun peek out at all. Night came early. All of the kids were running around in the dusk, and for once, Chonnie was amongst them. He was just looking for a good spot to hide. But those eyes found him. Those eyes, looking straight at his ojos verdes, and then they were gone. He almost didn't believe they were real. He looked all around until he found them again. They came up to him and spoke in a young girl's voice, "You, you're like me!"

"No," Chonnie said, "you are like me."

The little girl was wearing boy pants and a boy's shirt. She had long black hair tied into a trenza—indio style. To Chonnie, she looked very much indio, except for those eyes. Her skin was café con leche, very well stirred. And she looked like she was his age. She smiled at him. And he smiled back. A grin so big the corners of his lips almost touched his ears.

From that moment on, their eyes and their lives became forever entangled.

"My name is Inez. Short for Lilianez. My papá gave me that name to honor a long dead abuela I never met. Papá always said that I looked just like her. I don't know if that is true, but that's what he says. Abuela Inez, she took on los pinches rinches to defend her ranch. It wasn't much, just an acre. But it was her land. It was all that we had left after the Kings came. She would never give it up. She defended her land con huevos. It was just her and her papá, who was too old to work. She always carried the shotgun she got from a drifting vaquero that spent the night. They did more than sleep, Papá always says. I don't know what that means, but he always laughs. Abuela Inez only had ten shells because that was all she could afford. And she only fired it once on the night they came for her—Los Rinches. She wouldn't sell her land to the Kings and so they came like cucuys in the night," Inez stopped and looked out toward the sky. The clouds had broken, and she could see the stars. They seemed closer tonight, like they were listening.

"What happened next?" Chonnie asked noticing that she stopped her story short and stared off in silence.

Inez snapped out of her daze and continued.

"She didn't scream. That is how she resisted. There were five of them."

Chonnie swallowed hard. He didn't know exactly what she meant. He wasn't sure she did either. But they both knew it wasn't good. "Lo siento."

"My abuelo, Refugio, he works with your father. He told me the story. I was only ten."

"How old are you now?" Chonnie interrupted.

"Eleven," Inez said matter-of-factly.

Chonnie smiled, "I am eleven too."

"Great. Anyways, my abuelo told me this. I don't know

what it means. I hope that when I am older I will understand, but now I just know the words."

"What are the words?"

"Abuelo Refugio said: Our ojos verdes didn't come from some genetic misstep. They came from an act so hateful it has sorrowed the color green forever."

Chonnie stared at her in wonder. They were deep words.

"You see," Inez told Chonnie, "my abuelo was her son, and the man that raised my abuelo as his own was not his father. He always looked at him with different eyes than the others. My abuelo and me," Inez believed, "have the same eyes and the same sorrow. Our flesh and bones may be one thing, but our eyes are something different. How can something as beautiful as green eyes make me feel so shameful? That is why my abuelo Refugio gave me her shotgun. My abuela's shotgun. It is a reminder that I must stay strong, like her, even when I know I'm not. Everything depends on it."

Chonnie would hear several times throughout their juventud—even though they shared the same eyes, they weren't the same. His eyes came from his mother as hers before that. They had always been light-skinned. It was the Spanish blood, his mother always said. Chonnie knew it wasn't the Spanish blood though. He had heard the chisme. It was her abuela's affair with a local German boy back when Tejas was still Mexico. Forbidden love never uttered, never legitimized, just whispered.

It was his green eyes that first gave him the idea that he could pass for one of them. Years later, when Chonnie would study law at the University in Austin, he would realize how much those eyes could really deceive. The Anglos would often mistake him for one of them. It could have been the light skin or the light-colored hair, but he knew it was the eyes. They would just assume he was one of them—until he spoke. Then the rancho would spill out, betraying the deception with his ellos, pueses, and peros. Then they knew. He wasn't one of them. He was an imposter. He betrayed them. Appearing white when he was not. The worst betrayal of all. They made him feel disgust for his Mexicanness. It didn't take him long to change his accent to sound more like them. He Anglocized his name from Chonnie to Johnny. When he came home, it was as if an Anglo sheath covered his Mexican tongue. A sheath he forgot how to dislodge. Only his mother's piercing stare could dislodge the Anglo to free the Tejano in him.

Those ojos verdes in the Villas del Norte were rare. Mexican Tejanos and Mexicanos alike saw them as cancerous. The same way the Anglos viewed short thick curling jet black hair, thick lips, and wide nostrils. They were reminders of a past they wanted buried, forgotten, and ignored. Those eyes though, they were just too loud.

THE WIND THAT BLEW
BETRAYAL

The moon hung low on that unusual April night. It wanted a better look at the incident that would change everything. It was a beautiful night for injustice. For treachery. For a knot in the narrative thread. The skies were filled with so many stars that chased every cloud from the horizon. A breeze so cool, it could only have rolled off the ocean blew in that night. It rolled off the Gulf of Mexico. The breeze blew in carrying an Eastern chill. And like all things that came from the East, it never boded well for the West.

Chonnie sat high on his saddle because he forgot how to ride low. He hadn't ridden a horse in over five years, ever since he went away to get his law degree. He never thought that he would ever have to get back in the saddle. It was 1905 and the auto was quickly replacing the horse. In Austin, he saw roads being paved and autos parked where troughs used to water horses. He'd even had a chance to learn to drive once, but he couldn't master the clutch. Horses were worse for him. The horse he rode this night was the only horse that ever let him ride it. He'd had this horse for ten years. Inez had cared for Güero while he was gone. She called him Güero just to tease Chonnie. Everyone else had brown, grey, or black horses that blended into the landscape like shadows casting shadows. Güero, almost shimmered in the moonlight because of his white coat. He stood out for sure. Chonnie had to have the only horse that screamed: SHOOT ME! He had always chosen the wrong tool for the wrong chore. Tonight, was no different. He rode on the hunt looking for two bandidos that had stolen five steers from their rancho. Bandidos were a steady and growing problem as more Anglos started to move onto this land. His family's land. Tonight, though, wasn't about the Anglos. It was about the bandidos, rustlers—thieves from Old Mexico. They had been stealing cattle from local rancheros for months now and finally, the Rangers had a lead on where they were.

Chonnie had heard about the Texas Rangers moving into El Valle when he was away at school. His mother didn't trust them. They were all white boys from Arkansas and East Texas. Places, his mother said, where no Mexicano was welcome. But his 'apá, Daniel, had to trust them. They came to him with the governor's orders to protect Texas from "undesirables." Daniel Ruiz de Plata was always a law-abiding citizen, even though he heard la gente calling them, "rinches." Whispers of their misdeeds were louder than chicharas at night. But to Daniel, the Rangers had never done him wrong. So, when the Rangers came asking for his help in capturing bandidos stealing his cattle, he said yes. He even brought Macario and Chonnie. It was a decision that he would never live to regret.

"'Apá, ¿cuál es ése?" Macario shouted out bringing his horse to a stop.

"What is it?" Daniel answered back in English, so the Rangers would understand.

"Allá, I see something," Macario said pointing at the shadow of a tiny house with what looked like five steers.

Chonnie could barely see what they were looking at. He only saw shadows. and the Ranger's guns. The Ranger captain drew his big Dragoon pistol from its holster. The Ranger captain put his fingers to his lips and then cocked his head for his two deputies to follow him. Daniel started to go too, but the Captain gestured him to stay and he did. Daniel, Macario, and Chonnie looked at each other and waited for the signal from the Rangers. Macario had his Winchester out and ready. Daniel had his hand on his pistol which slept uneasily in its holster. Chonnie moved his coat from over his pistol and ever so gently touched the cold metal to make sure it was still there. He even adjusted the borrowed ranger badge over his chest. He tried to swallow but his mouth had gone dry and a lump began to form in his throat. Then the wind blew. The dust splashed over his face. He had no idea what was happening. All they could hear was the clop clop clop of horses' hooves moving away toward that little house. Strange, Chonnie thought, it's so quiet. No chicharas. Maybe they were waiting too.

Captain Pablo Honey wasn't really a captain. He was just a lieutenant. But the Mexicans didn't know that. They also didn't know that he wasn't chasing bandidos that night. He was setting a trap for the Plata boys. Pablo Honey was hired by the Kings to get the Plata's thousand-acre ranch for the expansion of the King Ranch. Pablo knew that John Kleberg, the current ranch manager and son-in-law to Richard King himself, wanted to buy that ranch for $50 an acre. But if that is what Kleberg really wanted, then he wouldn't have hired the boogeyman of Brazos County to do the deal. Pablo wasn't a dealmaker. He was a Texas Rangers and Rangers don't make deals with Mexicans. It was a Ranger's sworn duty to civilize Texas, and Mexicans were anything but. So, Pablo didn't even offer Daniel Plata a deal. He just hired men to steal his cattle and lead them into this trap. In order to get the deed to the Plata's ranch, all of the Plata's had to be dead.

"Hey!" a loud whisper broke the thick silence.

Daniel turned to see Blind Tommy Melon waving them over. Blind Tommy was one of Honey's most trusted men. He signaled for Macario and Chonnie to dismount and follow him. Daniel didn't know why they called him Blind Tommy. He saw just fine. Maybe it had to do with his young age or maybe he didn't see straight, which is probably why he only carried a shotgun. They followed him through the brush and into a clearing where Pablo Honey and four other men stood in front of the broke down house. No steers and no bandidos. Then Daniel heard the click. It came from behind.

"Move greasers. Your gooses are cooked."

Daniel thought about going for his gun, but Blind Tommy had the barrel of that scatter gun pointed at the back of Macario's head. There was no way Daniel was fast enough to draw before that shotgun went off, so he slowly raised his hands.

"Drop that heater, Chico, or I put this buckshot all through your brainpan," Blind Tommy said to Macario poking his head with the barrel, knocking Macario's hat off his head.

Chonnie just froze, waiting for instructions from his father and brother, but when he saw Macario drop his rifle, he knew it was over for them.

Blind Tommy pushed them forward into the clearing where the moonlight shone brighter than he had ever seen. What Blind Tommy didn't know was that the moon was at its brightest because it wanted a better look at what was about to go down.

The scene was set. The stars watched while the moon bathed its light. The house wasn't a house after all. It was an old weigh station—decrepit front door, window shutters barely holding on. A covered porch with creaky boards and two hitching posts. It was situated on an overgrown trail. It seems that the vaqueros had found a better trail to take their cattle. And like all things that sit, they gather dust and fall apart. The clearing around the old weigh station was still clear. All except the dirt and espinas. It was clear to everyone now that this was a special hideout for Honey and his men. This is where they brewed up the betrayal plan for the Platas. The plan required six men. Two disguised as bandidos. Two at Honey's side, for show, and the last one to get the drop on the unfortunate Plata's.

When Daniel, Macario, and Chonnie were dragged into the clearing, they saw the trap set in the sharpest white moonlight.

Blind Tommy was still behind them. Shotgun to their backs. Captain Honey stood on the steps of the wooden porch. One foot on each step, like a conquering hero, claiming this land for him and him alone. To his left was a man dressed as a bandido, and a ranger standing next to him, smoking. To Honey's right was another bandido. and another Ranger. The Plata's were certainly boxed in. It was a kill box.

"Now, I know what you're thinking," Pablo said to them slyly standing between two of his Rangers and the two bandidos, "What in tarnation is going on? I thought we were chasing bandidos for rustling cattle, but here we are. Ain't this a pickle. Tricked into this here well-laid plan. Like mice, or even better yet, cockroaches. Because that is what you people are…"

"Now, you listen here pendej…" Daniel shouted out as the anger spilled out of him, but not before Pablo's dragoon cut him off. The bullet knocked Chonnie clear off his feet, leaving him face first in the dirt. Macario tried to react and go for Chonnie but Blind Tommy knocked him upside the head. Before Macario knew it, he was on his knees. Daniel tried to move too, but several clicks stopped him for moving any further.

"I don't like to be interrupted when I'm just starting to monologue. Now, it looks like your youngest might still be breathing and if you want to keep it that way I wouldn't say another word until spoken to. Am I clear?"

Daniel seethed through his teeth but didn't say anything.

"It's okay," Pablo taunted Daniel, "you can answer. But let me just warn you, because I am a reasonable guy, if I don't like your answer, I will put a bullet right through his beautiful green eye. Now, answer me. Am I clear?"

"Sí," Daniel muttered under his breath.

"I'm sorry, I couldn't hear you. Did you just speak Mexican? This here is Texas and you will speak American when I talk to you. Do you understand?"

"Yes, Captain Honey."

"Well, that's better. And just because I am nice guy, I will take that answer for both questions. How's that for generous? Now, like I was saying before I was so rudely interrupted. I have led you here tonight for one reason and one reason only. John Kleberg offered myself and these here men lots of money to get you to sign over your land, and we aim to get paid. Now, he told me to offer you fifty dollars per acre, but I know that you will never sell him your land. It was granted to you by the King of Spain two hundred years ago and it has been passed down from father to son and father to son and so on. Right?"

"That is correct. My land is not for sale, not at any price, but especially not for fifty dollars an acre. That is an insult."

Pablo stepped toward Daniel and said, "You see, that is why we are in this predicament, right here and now. You are too proud to understand that this land ain't yours no more. It's ours—the Americans. We took it when we licked Mexico in that war all those years back. We just been slow to acquire it."

"We are Americans, too, and the treaty of Guadalupe Hidalgo guarantees my rights to my land," Daniel shot back.

"That's where you're wrong—so wrong. That treaty don't

hold no sway to white man's ambition. You ain't no white man, and only white men are Americans. We built this country. You're just in the way."

"The law doesn't see it that way."

"I understand why you feel that way, I really do. But that law ain't for you. It never was. It's for me and my kind."

Daniel gave Honey his hardest stare and said, "Really? We have more claim to this land them some güero with a Mexican name."

"You know something Daniel, I'm gonna give you that point. I ain't from around here. I'm from Brazos County. Around there I got a reputation. The negroes, they call me the Boogeyman. Do you know why?" Pablo said as he pointed the barrel of his Dragoon at Macario's crotch. "Now, be careful how you answer. Your sons huevos might pay the price."

"Because you come in the night and..."

"...I take their children first," Honey interrupted. He then lowered the gun and moved back to Daniel. "Now, let's get back to my Mexican name, since you brought it up. Pablo. How did a white boy like me get a name like Pablo? I ain't Mexican. Hell, I ain't even Spanish. But I have a Mexican name. Well, I'll tell you. My grandma, Petrina, she loved Mexicans. She loved them so much, she gave all of us kids, my brothers and sisters, Mexican nicknames like Jose for Joe and Maria for Mary. But for me, I was the youngest and my mamma passed when she was having me. So, I was raised and christened by my grandma, and so she named me Pablo. All official and everything."

"Your grandmother sounds like a decent lady," Daniel said trying to keep Honey engaged.

"But you want to know a secret, Daniel," Honey continued like he didn't hear a word Daniel said. "All my grandma's kids, my aunts and uncles all have blond hair, blue eyes, the works. But my Daddy, he has black hair and black eyes because my Grandma loved a mongrel dog like you and now we all tainted. My Daddy always got teased on. Always called a greaser, a half-spic, the whole works. But he never believed he was one. My grandma always said, it was because we had Italian blood in us. But when I was born, my grandma finally told him the truth, and you know what my Daddy did? He hung himself in the barn with the chickens and horses. So now I got Mexican blood in me too. So, I don't hate you. I am like you, but this here is business. Now, you got two choices here today. One, you give me everything you got, and I let you walk out of here with your two *hijos,* or I shoot you all dead and say those two bandits over there got the jump on us."

"And I suppose they just so happen to get away too, huh?" Daniel said.

"Well, nope, not really. I can't have two bandidos shoot up all of you here and just walk away. What kind of Rangers would that make us? No, those boys, got to die."

And just then, Pablo's two Rangers turned their guns on the "bandits" and shot them dead. They didn't even have a chance to hear the rest of Pablo's plan.

"You'll never get away with this, God will punish you," Daniel said in defiance.

33

"God! God don't care about no heathen Mexicans. He only listens to Christians…"

"We are Católicos," Daniel corrected him.

"No, sir," Pablo shot back at him, "Catholics are the worst kind of Christians. They serve a pope over their own Lord and Savior. That ain't Christian."

"The Pope is a servant of the Lord."

"I ain't here to have a theological discussion with you. I'm here to fulfill my legal duty and take what is rightfully ours. Now, the proposition still stands. Your land or your lives."

Daniel thought long and hard about his situation. He knew that whatever he decided, they were not going to make it out of there alive. "We are law-abiding citizens. Upstanding in the community. No one will believe that I just signed my land over to Kleberg. No matter how you spin it, the law won't just let you take my land."

"The law is changing, Daniel. That is why we are here. Sworn officers of the law, defending this land from all foreign threats. And you are foreign."

"We were here long before you gringos. You are the foreigners," Macario shouted out from his kneeling position.

Pablo looked down at Macario and said, "Well, now. Someone wasn't paying attention to the rules I clearly laid out a minute ago." Pablo leveled the barrel on Chonnie's prone body and fired. The bullet smashed into his chest and Chonnie just shuttered.

"Penalty for breaking the rules." Pablo leveled his dragoon at Macario's head and said, "You got one son left, so here's the deal,

Daniel. You sign over all of your land to John Kleberg or I end him right here and now."

Daniel begged for the life of his son, "No, Captain Honey, don't…"

"So, you'll sign over everything?" Pablo said cocking the hammer of his gun.

"Captain Honey, please…"

"One…"

"Okay, okay, I will do it."

Macario looked over at his father, shocked and angered and said, "No, 'Apá, don't give this rinche any…"

But Macario never got to finish. Pablo's bullet ate Macario's last words. The bullet also ate Macario, from his eyes to his ears, leaving no nose and only half teeth. Pablo had a habit of keeping his bullets starving until the right moment. Then he would release them. He would watch gleefully as his bullets devoured whoever was in their path. Macario was no different. The bullet that ate Macario though, wasn't alone. It was the pack leader that let loose all the other bullets in all the other rinche's guns. They tore through every one of the Plata's that night. Chonnie heard it all, lying on the ground. His breathing so shallow only the wind could hear it.

WAIT FOR ME

Inez Martinez de Plata sat in Washington Park, smoking a newly rolled cigarette. With half an eye, she watched her son, Bennie, as he played with three other children. They were all dressed in their Sunday best. It was an unusually cool April morning. She had just returned from San Antonio. She had met with Sister Margaret's School for Gifted Children about enrolling Bennie. Up until this year, they had been called a School for Wayward Girls. Because of new management, they started to take boys. They had always served prominent Texan families and the Platas were no exception. At these Catholic schools, they were taught to speak *proper English* and study with the best. Inez had grown up as a vaquera, doing vaquera things. Her family had always worked for ranchos. Going to school was never an option for them until the day they started working for the Platas. They had their own schoolhouse with Tía Carmen, the Platas' spinster, as the teacher for all the children.

When Inez had first met Chonnie, they were only ten. She thought he was a gringo, but then he spoke. And she saw that they both shared los ojos verdes. She knew that he was something different. They quickly became thick as thieves. Chonnie didn't get himself into trouble like los otros güercos. He liked books and daydreaming. He would help her with her reading and arithmetic, but she preferred chasing rabbits and hunting alligators in the resacas. She only ever saw one. It peeked its eyes above the waterline and then, just as quick as it had popped up, it was gone. Forever.

Inez tapped the side of her barely smoked cigarette, causing the long tower of ash to rain down on the ground below. She watched Bennie running around with the other kids and smiled. She remembered her favorite childhood hideout. It was an old abandoned house—overgrown and full of secrets. Inez called it "*The Monte.*" In that *monte,* they sacrificed dozens of toy indios and bandidos to the jungle in the imaginary war against COBRA, a "ruthless organization determined to rule the world." With the help of los bandidos rojos and whatever toys they could scrape together, they had entire armies in that overgrown lot beyond the grazing grounds. Inez once had a figure, Zartan, that was supposed to change color in the sunlight. That is what the advertisement in the back of the catalogue Chonnie had gotten from San Antonio had said. They scraped together twenty cents and sent away for it. When it arrived, they laid it on the ground and waited for the sun to do its magic. Zartan had other plans though, and stubbornly stayed the same color. Inez was left disappointed by its unwillingness to change colors. She kicked Zartan as hard as she could. She never saw him again. Inez thought he still might be there buried under fifteen years worth of dried cracked soil and other forgotten toys.

That monte was theirs. Inez and Chonnie's. It was where they went to get lost from homework, chores, and the world. She could still hear her grandfather yelling at them, *"bajen de allí,"* to get down from the tree because they could break an arm or worse. Never happened, but Chonnie did have an unfortunate encounter with a cactus that took several painful hours of removing needles from his backside.

As they grew up, she realized it was probably somebody's burnt down house. The owners probably with it. Los Rinches had always been there, like duendes in the shadows, waiting.

And then there was Macario. Inez knew he liked her, but he wasn't Chonnie. Macario was too serious. He was never a child. He never learned to play. Just to be the man that his father wanted him to be. Chonnie was different. He always had his head in the clouds and she was there with him. She never wanted to come down, but as they changed from boy and girl to man and woman, their friendship grew into something else.

Macario hated how close she was with Chonnie. Inez saw his jealousy in the way he would treat Chonnie. He tried hard to show her he was much stronger and better than Chonnie, but she never felt anything for him. Not like Chonnie. Macario took all his frustration out on Chonnie every chance he got. Macario was better than Chonnie at almost everything and he rubbed Chonnie's face in it every chance he got. Chonnie never seemed to really get angry at Macario. He just said that his brother was his brother and that was the way he was. He always brushed it off. But Inez would sometimes catch Chonnie alone in the monte, crying. She never comforted him though. She just watched quietly and slipped away to let him be. She never knew why she didn't comfort him. It was something that would always haunt her.

"Wait for me," she muttered under her breath and tossed her cigarette to the ground. "Wait for me," were the last words that Chonnie had said to her before he left her on that clear August night—so sticky, so hot, just like those words. They stung her everytime she heard them. They had broken her heart. Chonnie had broken her heart. He had chosen his mother's orders over their love.

On that night, she was ready. He was not. She blamed Herlinda because she never wanted Chonnie to stay. Herlinda wanted her son to be a lawyer. He wasn't brave like Macario. He never stood up to her. He just sunk his head low and obeyed, every single time. He wanted to do right by his family. Inez knew that. Even if it cost Chonnie the one thing he wanted more than anything.

When Inez and Chonnie were thirteen, they had gotten engaged in secret. They swore that they would marry each other when they were old enough. They waited until after Inez's quinceñera, and announced it to Chonnie's parents. Herlinda shut their engagement down without a consideration for Chonnie or Inez. He was not to marry one of their worker's daughters. Inez's parents, Raul and Claudia Martínez, were happy to hear about their love, but they had no choice but to agree with the Doña of the house. Inez and Chonnie were so upset that they decided they were going to run off together. Damn their families to hell!

They were supposed to meet at the monte. Inez showed up

with a large potato sack. It had one extra dress, a couple of pieces of bread, and uncooked beans. She waited and started to get worried when she spotted something dug into their favorite tree. It was a note that read, "Wait for me." Inez breathed a sigh of relief. She waited, but he never came. She waited all night until her heart finally believed he wasn't coming. She walked back home. Each step becoming heavier and heavier. No tears. Just the heaviness of a heart ready to burst. She returned home to the news that Chonnie had left late that night. He wasn't coming back for five years.

The man that was there to pick up the pieces of her broken heart was Macario. That was what she told herself when she agreed to marry him. Macario was always there. He never hurt her like Chonnie. Maybe because she wouldn't let Macario close enough to really know her. She never would.

Inez felt a tear forming behind her eyes, so she stood up and straightened her dress. "Bennie, come on. We have to go."

Adán and Ernesto were late picking them up to take them back to the rancho. Adán Peña and Ernesto Garcia were the Plata's best drivers. They always picked up the family from the train station. Inez dug a silver pocket watch from her waist pocket and checked the time. Something was wrong. They were never late. Their train had arrived an hour ago and Inez thought they were probably early, so she took Bennie to the park to play.

After a good look around the station, she saw something that made her heart skip a beat. She saw Sheriff Jaime Santos walking toward her with señora Garcia in tow. Señora Garcia was Ernesto's mother and the rancho's best cook. The sheriff took off his hat

41

when he reached her. What he had to say brought her hand to her mouth. She had no words. She fell back onto the bench. "All of 'em?" was all that could escape her lips. Words so devastating that all she could do was repeat them, "All of 'em?"

SWALLOWED

That bullet swallowed him whole but it wouldn't kill him. He felt trapped like gunpowder waiting to explode. He struggled to breathe. Each breath becoming more shallow than the last. The dull pain rumbled through his chest as the second shot ricocheted off the borrowed rinche badge. His life didn't flash before his eyes like it was supposed to. He was just trapped in the moment. Swallowed by the weight of it. Breath seemed to abandon him when he needed it the most. He didn't know which breath was going to be his last, so he counted. One. Two. Three. Four. And then on five, he stopped.

He let his thoughts just flow out of him. His mother. The train ride home. Inez in the barn. The last night before Austin. Before she married his brother. Before the birth of his nephew. That last night was all that kept him there. In a space where there is nothing but dark and cold. The wind swept him further and further away...and then...a sound...he heard something. A voice. *Twenty-five years and my life is still—trying to get up that great big hill of hope—for a destination. What's going on?* It was his voice, but it wasn't. Then, more voices. Arguing.

"They're all dead," one voice shot from the darkness, "we've got to go."

"No, I won't let Honey escape this time. Not this time," a second voice shouted.

Then Chonnie felt something deep inside of his chest. Something bubbling up. And then a cough…

Sometimes Tal'dos saw. Sometimes Tal'dos saw too far. This had been the white elephant sitting in the corner of his life. That was why Tal'dos saved Chonnie on the night the moon hung low. Tal'dos saw what was to come—like the moon and the stars. He needed to make sure it happened. For everyone's sake.

Bass, on the other hand, was not so sure. But Bass knew that he couldn't just leave him there to die. He had a badge after all. If forty years of marshaling had taught him anything, it was that you can't leave a brother in blue behind.

I realized quickly, when I knew I should—that the world was made up of this brotherhood of man—for whatever that means. And so I cry sometimes when I'm lying in bed—just to get it all out, what's in my head. And I, I am feeling—a little peculiar.

"You hear that?" Bass asked as they carefully loaded Chonnie's bullet-ridden body on to their hackcart.

"It's just his soul singing," Tal'dos answered back.

"No, I think he's trying to say something," Bass lied his head gently down and leaned his ear close to Chonnie's mouth.

Tal'dos slid himself onto the cart and asked, "What's he

saying?"

Bass, looking puzzled, pulled his head back and said, "He said, all of 'em."

"All of 'em? He must be asking if they're all dead. Don't tell him nothing."

"No, this boy just said, 'He said, all of 'em.'"

"What does that mean?" Tal'dos said sounding confused.

"I ain't got a clue, but we got to get him out of here or this boy's gonna die," Bass said as he closed the tailgate to their covered hackcart.

Tal'dos stopped for a second and whispered, "Bass," putting a finger to his lips.

But it was too late, Bass heard the clicking back of a shotgun hammer. "Well, what the hell we got here?" said a short mustachioed flopping hat-wearing cowboy with a shotgun shining in the moonlight.

Bass put his hands up and turned to see a disappeared Tal'dos. "Easy, son."

"What you doing here, old timer?" said the short mustachioed, floppy hat-wearing, cowboy with a shotgun.

"Son, my name is Bass Reeves and I am a duly appointed federal marshal. Who are you?" Bass said stepping away from the hackcart and toward the shiny shotgun.

"Bass Reeves? I heard of you. You that lawman they all fear up in Oklahoma..."

"Paris, Texas," Bass corrected him.

"Paris what?"

"Texas. It's a town near the Oklahoma and Arkansas line."

"I thought Paris was in France."

"It is, and it's also in Texas."

"Well, whatever," short, mustachioed cowboy said getting flustered, "What you doing here anyway? You far from North Texas here."

Bass knew this little cowboy was left there to keep guard. Bass didn't know how they missed him, but they did. There was something wrong with this situation, so Bass continued, "What's your name, son?"

"What's my name? Look, old timer, I'm a duly appointed Texas Ranger and you ain't got no jurisdiction here."

"You still gotta have a name, don't you? Come on. From one lawman to another. What's your name?" Bass said taking a step closer.

"My name is Walter Waterson, but they call me Slim," Slim said, not dropping the shotgun a centimeter.

"Slim, huh, I can see that. Now, why don't you put that shotgun down? We both blue bloods here."

"What you got in the hack there?" Slim gestured with the barrel toward the cart.

"Oh that, that is one of your fellow Ranger's all shot to hell. We were just taking him to get some help," Bass said taking one more step closer.

"Fellow Ranger, there ain't no Ranger's shot. Just…" and then Slim's eyes widened. He realized there was still one left alive. "Listen here Bass Reeves, you got to give me that boy. He ain't no

Ranger. He's a bandido we was tracking."

"But he's wearing one of your badges? And he look white, just like you, and green eyes to boot. You sure he ain't one of yours?" Bass said, knowing he smelled metaphorical bullcrap on Slim.

"He stole it. He's a dirty greaser."

"Oh, is he?"

"Yeah, so hand him over and you can be on your way," Slim said inching his way left of Bass towards the hackcart.

"Can I tell you something, son?" Bass said catching Slim off guard.

"What?"

"I've arrested fourteen hundred men marshaling and in that time, I've learned two things."

"Yeah, what's that?"

"I know when a man's got a guilty conscience hanging on him. And you, son, are draped in it. Your lying. You ain't no lawman."

"I ain't lying. I's a duly appointed Texas Ranger."

"That may be true, but you ain't no lawman," Bass said, seething through his teeth. His hands still up.

"I am the law here," Slim said still moving around Bass toward the hackcart.

"You want to know the second thing I learned is?"

Slim stopped and thought for a second, not sure what was going on, "Sure."

"I learned to make sure that the man you're tracking is alone."

"What?" but before Slim realized what he meant, the shotgun was knocked from his hands. In its place was a strange silver star stuck in his hand. Blood poured out like a leaky faucet. Then everything went black for Slim, because the butt of a rifle landed right between his eyes.

"Took you long enough," Bass said, putting his hands down, "My arms were getting tired. What were you waiting for anyway? The 4th of July? Jesus. Tie him up and take him with us. He could be useful."

Tal'dos looked upset, "Why do I got to tie him up?"

"You knocked him out, you get to tie him up," Bass said, moving to take his seat at the head of the cart.

"Somehow, I think your logic only ever works to benefit you," Tal'dos said, kicking Slim's hands out from under him.

"I didn't create it. Logic just is. Come on, hurry up. This boy's dying."

Tal'dos shook his head and tore his shuriken from Slim's hand.

And so, I wake in the morning and I step outside—and I take a deep breath and I get real high. And I—scream from the top of my lungs. What's going on? And I say, hey yeah yeah, hey yeah yeah. I said hey. What's going on?

"Boy's singing again," Bass said sounding upset.

"He's on the shore of the afterlife. Let him sing," Tal'dos said stringing up poor old Slim.

THIS TRAIN

How long had he lived in Brownsville? How long had it taken him to gain these people's trust? How long had he worked to bring this city into the future? Progress is what this place needs, James Stillwell thought as he walked down Adams street to his office on this crisp April morning. The only thing keeping this place from progress is the Mexican Tejanos that held onto their antiquated Spanish land grants with a death grip. Even though he had helped several of these families fight the U.S. government, these patrones stood in the way of real progress—American progress. He knew that these patrones were so set in their ways that they blocked every single attempt to bring the railroad to these villas. But now with the completion of the St. Louis, Brownsville, Mexico Railway, it was too late. Modern America was here, and with it, real wealth. Agricultural wealth. White wealth.

Stillwell turned the corner of 10th and Adams, and out front stood Zefrino Puente. Zeferino was one of the landowners that John Kleberg had successfully bought. *La gente* called them Kineños. It carried as much weight in the Mexicano community as

49

Benedict Arnold for the Americans or Malinche for the Mexicanos. He was wearing his long dirty dust jacket covering his nice Sunday suit and a dusty tan hat that drooped over his forehead. He also had the butt of a burnt-out cigar hanging out of his mouth. He looked like his mother hadn't dress him that morning.

"Zeferino, what are you doing here on this fine Monday morning?" James said a little annoyed.

"Jim, we have to talk about what happened with the Platas," Zeferino said seething with fear and anger in his words.

James pulled his keys from his pocket and started to unlock his front door. "Jesus, Zefe, you want the whole town to hear you? Let's talk inside."

James opened the door wide for Zeferino to enter, and enter he did. His boot spurs clanked loudly on the hard wood floors with every step—and because of his girth, he stepped extra hard. "I don't like what happened. Not one bit," Zeferino said as soon as he was inside.

"I don't like it either. Look, have a seat. It looks like you are going to blow your top," James said gesturing to a seat directly across from a big wooden desk. Zeferino sat down hard and James worked to open the shutters to his office to let the light in.

"Jim, if this is the way that business is going to be done then…"

"…then what?" James said cutting him off, "you'll stop taking our money? You'll confess to the authorities?" James laughed.

"Maybe I will," Zeferino countered.

James stopped opening the shutters and walked over to his

desk and sat in his oversized leather chair. "Zefe, if you even try to turncoat, the Platas won't be the only ones who will know the fury of those *Mexican bandits*," James countered.

"Jim, Kleberg wouldn't. He needs me. He needs my men."

Jim leaned back, "Zefe, have you been paying attention to what's been going on around here? The Rangers are on the King's payroll now. There are more and more of them coming down every day because they know that we pay, and we pay well. Those government salaries don't amount to squat—but Kleberg, he pays very very well. So, how long do you think we will need you?"

"Those güeros can't do what I can. I have spies in the local communities. Those boys stick out like sore thumbs."

"That we do!" came a loud booming voice from behind James Stillwell.

Zeferino looked up to see a tall, long blond haired and bearded güero. Piercing black eyes, black hat, long black jacket, and a dragoon pistol the size of his leg strapped to his hip. "Who are you?" Zeferino asked startled.

"My name is Pablo Honey. I am a lieutenant for the Special Ranger Unit of the Texas Rangers, and I'm the man that's gonna get you," long pause, "eventually," another long pause, "if we don't get your continued cooperation."

Zeferino swallowed hard and looked back at James Stillwell. "Jim, I am not here to back out of our deal. I'm just concerned about these rinches' tactics."

"Zefe, I completely understand," James said trying to calm him down, "These Ranger boys do like to make a hell of a state-

ment. But something that brutal can't be done again without draw-
ing too much unwanted attention. You hear me, Honey?"

"I hear you Jim, but you can't deny it was effective. The
other patrones are falling in line now," Honey said, pulling a freshly
rolled cigarette from his breast pocket. He lit it with a silver lighter
that had the letter "P" engraved on it.

Zeferino recognized the lighter as Daniel Plata's and said,
"Where did you get that lighter?"

"Off that dead Mexican papa. He ain't gonna need it anymore."

Zeferino was horrified but didn't say anything. He just
turned back to James Stillwell at his desk. Stillwell didn't look horrified at all. James looked annoyed. "Do we have a problem here,
Zefe?"

Zeferino swallowed hard and said, "No, no hay problema
aquí."

"We still simpatico then?"

Zefe got up grunting the entire way up. "Yes, Jim. But
please, let's not have a scene like that again."

James took a cigarette from a nicely ornate box on his desk
and Pablo leaned forward with the lighter. James sucked in the
tobacco and said, "There's no need for anything like that anymore,
Zefe. Not unless someone decides to stop doing their part."

Zeferino looked to Pablo who had a half grin on his face
and back to James. Zeferino just nodded his head and walked toward the front door.

"You know something Zefe, when we were first cooking

this up, you didn't seem to be upset about Daniel Plata getting a belly full of lead," James said ashing his cigarette.

"It's not Daniel I care about. But why Herlinda and Carmen? All of those people at the Plata rancho."

"We had to get all of 'em," Pablo answered.

"Zefe, there can't be anyone left to claim rights to that land. They all had to go," James said, trying to reassure Zeferino.

"But the women?"

"It's a dirty business, but in the end—progress." And just when he said that, the train whistle blew. "Just like that train. It's bringing more and more progress to this area. This train is everything, and you are a part of that, Zefe."

Zefe nodded one last time, "Yeah, I know," he said as he twisted the door knob and exited.

"Lots of money to be made," James shouted as the door shut. He didn't know if Zeferino heard him or not, but he got the message loud and clear.

"Is that fat Mexican gonna be a problem?" Honey said, moving from behind James to the seat directly in front of the desk.

"No, Zefe is a loyal dog. Always has been. He doesn't have the guts to do anything but what Kleberg tells him. Besides, he loves money more than loyalty to his people."

"I don't really care. I'm just here to collect my money and then I'll be out of here."

"But your work ain't done."

"What do you mean? I got 'em all."

James snubbed out the last remaining bit of his cigarette

and leaned forward, "You missed two."

"Who?"

"Lilianez, Macario's wife, and his boy, Benicio."

"We killed all the Platas at the rancho."

"They weren't there. They were in San Antone, and they got back two days ago."

"So, I'll kill them too."

"No, you can't now. Too much attention. The massacre has made the papers. We got to wait for the heat to blow over."

Pablo squinted his eye in frustration, "How long do I have to wait?"

"At least six months. It takes at least that for the titles to be formalized in Benicio's name."

"I've got to be here another six months? What am I gonna do here for six months? It ain't exactly Houston."

"Go to Matamoros. Get your pencil dipped. Enjoy the local delicatessens. In the meantime, I'm sure there will be work. I'll call on you."

"Alright, but I just got to ask one question."

"What's that?"

"What do you get out of this? I mean, this seems an awful lot of killing for just some greasers' land."

James leaned back and smiled, "It's about progress. I've lived here for over twenty years and I've seen this place run by these patrones and nothing changes. Not for hundreds of years. The nobles still have all the power and the peasants work for them. It's been like that forever. But me, I'm a self-made man. I am the

American Dream. I believe in progress and I want to change this place. I want to drag it into the 20th Century with the rest of America."

Pablo scoffed, "So, you want your name on the side of a building?"

"No, Mr. Honey, I want to own this town. That train is my key to that dream, and no Patrón is gonna stand in my way."

NEVER TRUST THE STARS

How many times have the stars betrayed us? How many times has the sun set and let evil deeds be done? Only the moon as its witness. But the stars—these tricksters of light. Dead long ago. Now, ghosts of their former selves. Trickling dim light on the world, on us, and on that night of betrayal, they shone their brightest. The trick this time was not for evil deeds, but for something else. For defiance. For on that night of bright light, a bullet decided to change its path—and with it, history.

How many bullets have ever been fired? How many have mattered? Really mattered? to the course of human life? Maybe a dozen. But the .44 caliber bullet that was loaded into the chamber of Pablo Honey's Colt Dragoon was tired of having its fate decided by gunpowder and the laws of physics. It was tired of seeing its brothers and sisters being used to cause so much tragedy, so much death in the world. It decided like no bullet before it, to stop. To not kill. But instead, to give birth to life. A new life with new purpose. So, on that night—the night of betrayal, that bullet conspired with the stars to trick the world, and so it did.

Hiro Akiyama sat on the beach, deep in meditation. Eyes closed, legs crossed, elbows balanced on knees. A cup of saki in his right hand. Taking small sips. It was a steady buzz that he was after. Not drop dead drunk like he had seen the Anglos in bars, or the Mexicans at their fiestas. They had not mastered the true art of inebriation, but Hiro was certainly on the path to finding it. His sister, Itsuko, had tried several times to hide the Saki from him, but she was never successful. Itsuko was not trained in the art of Ninjutsu and she was not very good at hiding things. Hiro knew all her hiding places. She would not have done well as an assassin. She was a farmer. Just like everyone in their family.

Except Hiro—who had chosen, at a young age, to become samurai. But he was not of noble birth. Therefore, he was shut out of samurai training forever. But then, he had found—or more accurately—he had been found by Fūma Kotarō, the legendary Shinobi ninja master. Fūma Kotarō's greatest achievement was the killing of Hattori Hanzō. It was a kill that had gone down in history like no other. And Fūma Kotarō had chosen young Hiro to be his apprentice.

The training took years. Most of his childhood. Until his nineteenth birthday when he was sent on his first mission. The first they say, is the hardest. But it wasn't. Not for Hiro. It happened much faster than he anticipated—with poisoned tea for a trade minister's wife, and a slit throat for the trade minister.

Hiro raised his cup to his lips and felt the pang again in his right shoulder blade. That was years ago, he thought. When he was more than a crippled old man living thousands of miles from his home. A burden to his sister and her two daughters. He couldn't even fish. But she wanted him by her side anyway. Japan was filled with too many ghosts, Itsuko told him. But this Mexican-United States borderland did nothing but make him drink even more. The climate was why they moved there. They originally arrived through San Francisco, but the climate was too wet and cold. The hatred for Japanese was too dangerous for Itsuko and her children. Hiro could not fight like he used to. He was no protection. Not anymore. So Itsuko took in with a colony heading for Texas. They landed in Houston and found more hatred there. Another colony headed down to Port Isabel, on the coast, where it was quiet, and the Mexicans welcomed them.

They had been there twelve years now, and Itsuko was doing well selling shrimp to the local businesses. Their boat, the Oichi, was all they had in this colony. But at least, Hiro thought, they were by the beach. And that made everything okay. That and Tal'dos.

"Hiro!" Tal'dos shouted for him from off in the distance.

Speak of the demon, Hiro thought as he rose from his seated position. He downed the last of the Saki and turned to see Tal'dos with a tall black man, a hackcart, and trouble brewing in the air.

"What trouble have you brought me?" Hiro said advancing through the shifting sands.

"Purpose," was all Tal'dos said.

"Purpose?" Hiro raised an eyebrow to Bass.

Bass shrugged his shoulders and said, "I don't know about purpose, but we got ourselves a real double-cross here. Something bad is going on down here in these borderlands."

Hiro nodded, "Indeed."

"Remember you said that the wind was primed for deception," Tal'dos pointed toward the sky.

Hiro looked inside the cart. He saw one man hogtied and struggling, and another half-dead and said, "Yes, I remember, but it was the stars, not the wind. And you can't trust the stars."

WHO LIVES, WHO DIES, WHO TELLS YOUR STORY

It was like swimming through air, but without arms, without legs—without a body. It was just a song sung cruelly. More of a whistle, actually. A song he couldn't quite place. But it sounded like a train whistle trying to keep rhythm with the roar of the railway. It was his trip back home. It was a dream that was so real. It was a memory wrapped in gravity, pulling him down to somewhere worse than hell.

"Mijito, you're home," it was his mother, looking a bit older than he remembered. A streak of white in her brownish red hair. He stepped off the cart and let her hug him hard.

"Amá, it's good to see you," he said like he had done this scene before.

"Come, get something to eat. You look like you haven't eaten at all up there at your fancy school," his mother pulled into the main house, which was a large hacienda with too many rooms for the four of them. "I have calabaza con pollo, just cooked up."

Calabaza con pollo was his favorite, and she knew it. The smell of fresh tortillas being made filled every inch of the house and his every cell. As he walked further into the house, something happened—a cough. He coughed and coughed and coughed. He pulled a handkerchief from his pocket, covered his mouth, and pulled it away to see a silver bullet. This was not as he remembered this day.

"Aye, Chonnie, you look so guapo in your new suit and hat," it was his tía Carmen with her sunflower apron covered in harina. She wiped her hands on a towel tucked into the string of her apron. She walked over to him and hugged him. "So, how does it feel to be *un abagado* now?"

"I'm not one just yet. I still have to take the Bar," but even as he said these words, déjà vu hit him like a glitch in the matrix. Then the telephone rang.

"Tía, when did we get a telephone?"

"¿Qué?" she said, as if she didn't hear the ringing getting louder and louder.

"The telephone ringing, YOU DON'T HEAR THAT?" he said, trying to talk over the loud ringing sound. Then he realized it wasn't a ring, it was that cruel song again.

"Chonnie," the saying of his name caused the ringing to stop. "Hi," he turned around to see Inez looking different than when he left all those years ago. She was fuller in all the right places. Breasts. Hips. Butt. But she was still small. It was Mayan blood that kept her from growing past five feet two inches. When she walked over to him, it was the first time he realized that his six feet two inches towered over her. Yet, somehow, he seemed so small compared to her. "It's good to see you. It's been a long time."

Chonnie could not tell what was behind her tone. Was it hurt? Was it anger? Was it longing? He tingled all over and felt weightless. "Inez, you look...well," he had to autocorrect himself before the wrong words came out. She was his brother's wife after all, and no longer the Inez he left standing in their monte all those years ago.

Just then, a little boy of no more than nine years ran up to Inez and pulled at her dress, "Amá, can I please go out and play with the Salinas', PLEASE!?"

Inez tore her gaze away from Chonnie and looked down at her son, "Bennie, no, you know we are leaving for San Antonio. I don't want you getting all dirty."

"Ahh, ma, por favor. I won't get dirty. I promise."

"No. I said, no," she said with the sternness that only a mother could muster. Bennie went quiet with fear. Then a second later, in a softer voice, Inez said, "Bennie, I want to introduce you to your tío Chonnie."

Bennie looked over to a dumbfounded Chonnie. Chonnie waved and said, "Hi, I'm your tío. I've been away..."

"...at school. I know, *mi mamá* told me," Bennie cut him off.

Chonnie bent over and extended his hand for shaking. Bennie looked up at his mother and she gestured for him to shake his tío's hand. Bennie reluctantly made his way to his tío and placed his tiny hand in Chonnie's. For the first time, he saw that Bennie had green eyes. "He has green eyes, too?" Chonnie said sounding a little surprised.

"Just like us...just like me," Inez said autocorrecting herself and hoping Chonnie didn't hear her.

"Owww. Owww," Bennie began to scream, "Let go of me."

Chonnie looked down. He realized he was squeezing Bennie's hand, but he couldn't stop. Just then, Inez rushed over and pulled their hands apart. Chonnie started to hear that cruel song again. He looked down at his hand. That silver bullet was still there. It looked like a disfigured mushroom.

Chonnie, feeling horrible, looked up at Inez and said, "I'm sorry. I don't know what came over me."

"What's wrong with you?" she said poking him in the chest.

"Oww," he said, "That really hurt."

"What? This?" she said poking him even harder.

"Stop that."

The house setting melted away like a hologram short circuiting.

"Why? You left me there. Alone," Inez said, but her voice was different. Lower and darker.

She poked again.

"Inez, please. I'm sorry."

"How could you? I loved you and you just left," another hard poke.

Chonnie finally looked down and saw a Texas Ranger badge on his chest with the center of the star bent inward. "Huh, that doesn't look right." He looked back at Inez, but it wasn't her, it was Pablo Honey with a pair of pliers coming at his chest. "No, please, no."

Then the cruel song got louder: *Let me tell you what I wish I'd known. When I was young and dreamed of glory. You have no control. Who lives? Who dies? Who tells your story? Time... Who lives?... time... Who dies?...time... Who tells your story?*

"I got it!," Hiro shouted as he pulled the .44 caliber from Chonnie's chest. "It only took three tries."

"Three? That was more like five," Tal'dos teased Hiro.

Bass stood in the back watching the operation game happening and singing under his breath, "Who lives? Who dies? Who tells your story?"

"Bass," Tal'dos said, "we got it. He's gonna live. You can stop singing that song."

"It's a great tune," Bass shot back.

"It's a show tune."

"It's still a good tune."

Hiro dropped the bullet in a metal bucket and wiped the blood from his hands. "He'll be fine...eventually."

"What happens now, Tal'dos?" Bass said walking over to Chonnie's unconscious body on their makeshift operating table. It smelled like shrimp, fish guts, and blood.

"Now, Bass, the real work begins," Tal'dos said smiling.

"You think he's gonna lead you to Pablo Honey? The boy's half-dead," Bass said not so sure.

"I think he will do more than that," Tal'dos said finally sure of the path ahead.

"How do you know that?" Bass said still skeptical.

"I've seen it. We are going to train him."

"We?" Hiro said sipping on a cup of Saki he pulled from seemingly nowhere.

"Yes," Tal'dos said, "All of us."

"This ain't what I signed up for, Tal'dos," Bass said shaking his head.

"But this is the deal. You owe me," Tal'dos guilted him. "But first, we have a rinche to turncoat."

FATHER OF MINE

It was the sound that was the most unnerving. The sound of a knife scraping wood. Constant, steady, and unknown. That was the sound of a future that Slim did not want. It was the sound of his father cutting wood to perfection, for a rocking chair, for some rich prick's kitchen cabinets. He swore that he would never work for the pennies they paid his father for pure artistry. Those rich bastards didn't care that his father worked long hours into the night, just to get every single detail correct. They just wanted their furniture pieces quick and cheap. He hated all of 'em. His father especially. For not being man enough to charge more. For not standing up to those Eloi. They might have been Morlocks, like that Wells novel called 'em. But at least Morlocks ate Eloi—but Slim's Dad was not even that to them. He was too kind, too gentle. And that is why Slim couldn't follow in his father's footsteps. He hated Denton anyway. Too settled of a city. Too cosmopolitan for his tastes. He wanted to be one of those legends in those dime store novels. Jesse James, Wyatt Earp, and of course, his favorite, John Wesley Harding.

Scrape. Scrape. Scrape. That sound kept him in the moment—tied to a chair in the middle of a room that smelt of fish. He couldn't see anything. They had bagged his head when the Indian had sucker punched him, while the old black one distracted him. He thought he was dead for sure. Hogtied in the back of that hackcart. Instead, there he was. Still tied, still breathing. But that sound. The scraping wouldn't quiet itself. It just kept on until… The bag came off his head and he could see. He was in some sort of fishmonger's cutting room. A table filled with cut up fish guts and shrimp tails, hooks and poles hanging on the wall.

"Do you like this?" said the Indian sitting across from him. There was something different about this Indian. He was dressed in a plain white shirt. He had a black vest that seemed to be made of beads. It had a beaded white cross over each breast. Down the stomach on the left side was a beaded woman—on the right was a beaded man. Seemed a lot of detail for a vest. "Hey Slim, you with me?"

Slim looked at the Indian's face. He had very smooth features. "Yeah, I hear 'ya." The Indian held up a carved man in front of him. It wasn't very good. "Looks like a five-year-old did it," Slim said insulted.

The Indian pulled it back and looked at it hard and long, "Well, it was my first doll."

"If you're gonna kill me, just go ahead and do it," Slim said, sounding tough.

"Kill you? Oh no. I don't want to kill you. I need you Slim," the Indian said, setting the little carved man on the edge of the cutting table.

"What for?" Slim asked.

"I thought you would never ask. You see, I need you to lead me to Pablo Honey."

Slim scoffed and said, "No way that's happening. We don't sell out our own."

"Oh, you don't do you? Well, we'll see about that. But before we get started, let me introduce myself. My name is Tal'dos Unahu, son of Mape'l Blue Flower of the Carrizo, and Running Coyote of the Muskogee. Now, I usually mention my mother first because my father wasn't much of a father. Too much time hunting outlaws on the plains, I guess. I don't know. He was a son of a… anyway, I'm getting off topic. Let's talk about *your* father."

Slim tried very hard not to let Tal'dos see the flinch in his eye. How did he know he was thinking about his father? Slim thought. "What do you care about my father?"

"Your father was a real artist, wasn't he? A master craftsman."

"How do you know my father?"

"I don't. But *you* did."

"What does that mean?"

Tal'dos pulled a small wooden horse from his vest pocket and placed it on the table. Tal'dos set it next to the crappy one he had just carved. "This is expert craftsmanship—real artistry. Did you do this?"

Slim stayed quiet.

"That's okay. I know your daddy did this. It's got precision that screams years and years of practice. And looking at your hands—you don't have the hands to do this kind of work. Too much time spent pulling triggers and playing cards. Those are idle hands," Tal'dos said, sliding the wooden horse close to the edge of the table.

Slim kept his lips sealed.

"Is your Daddy proud of you? In your profession? or was he disappointed that you didn't follow in his footsteps?" Tal'dos said, sliding the wooden horse to the edge of the table.

"I ain't gonna tell you nothin'," Slim seethed through his teeth.

"Alright then. I guess then…" Tal'dos didn't finish his words. He simply slowly pushed the horse until it teetered on the edge. Then right when it was starting to fall…

"Don't—don't do it," Slim couldn't help it.

Tal'dos let it fall but caught it with his other hand. He placed it back on the table.

Slim started talking, "I hated my father. He never stood up for himself. He was a sorry case of a man. He let those rich fools treat him like a common houseboy. His work deserved better. But he never…he never stood up for himself. And I swore I would never be like him. Is that what you wanted to hear?"

"I hated my father too. He died recently. I've been having trouble processing that because he was the worst kind of father. The worst kind of husband to my mother. And what he did still sticks in my boot like a rock you can never get out," Tal'dos said leaning back in his chair.

"What happened to him?" Slim asked genuinely.

"He died of too much drink. Whiskey killed him, but not before he killed my mama."

"Sorry to hear that. What did he do? Beat her to death? Indians tend to be…you know, savage," Slim said goading Tal'dos.

"Oh no, he did something far worse than that. You see, he wasn't full-blooded Indian. He was half-white man. His father was a white man, ex-confederate soldier. The two parts of him were always warring. But *you* know, it was the white man that made him a bastard. Like all white men—they make promises, then break them."

"Go to hell, Injun. This land was nothing before we got here," Slim said struggling against his restraints.

"Arrogant too. Thank you for reminding me. You take our land, and then try like hell to kill us. But you can't, and my father couldn't kill the Indian in him. But boy, he tried."

"Does this story have a point?"

"What happened to your father, Slim?"

"What do you mean?"

"Why did you stop being a carpenter and choose to take up the gun?"

Slim didn't like where this was going. Did he really know? "I wasn't ever a carpenter."

"But you apprenticed under him, didn't you? Something happened, though. What was it?" Tal'dos pressed him.

"What does it matter? How does this help you find Pablo? What does anything about my father have to do with this? Here! Right now!" The words exploded out of Slim before he realized he said them.

Tal'dos let him scream. It was the beginning of the breaking. Tal'dos knew that it was now time for step two. Tal'dos reached into his other breast pocket and pulled out a small wooden bird.

"This is yours, isn't it? You carved this." Tal'dos ran his finger over the head and down its back. "This doesn't have the same skill as the horse. So, this has to be your work. There is talent here for sure, but you are just out of practice." He placed it next to the horse.

Slim locked his gaze at his bird. It was a hummingbird. He worked on it when him and his troop camped at night. It helped him sleep—the simple repetition of the carving. "Have you ever read that book, The Time Machine by H.G. Wells?" Slim asked.

Tal'dos simply shook his head and said, "No, I have not."

"It's about a guy, a scientist, who builds this machine that lets him travel through time. When he tests it, he ends up years in the future. The world is made up of two kinds of people there. The Eloi and the Morlocks. The Eloi are all prissy and pampered. Wearing togas and stuff like that. They just live off the land, happy, and have everything their hearts desire. But then there are these Morlocks, ugly creatures that live underground. They are the ones that make everything for the Eloi to live off of. All the Eloi have to do is give up one of their own to be eaten by the Morlocks every so often. It's the balance that has to be maintained. Well, my father for all his talent, always thought he was an Eloi. These Dallas elites that he made his crafts for, they knew the truth. We were just Morlocks.

He would never be one of them. I saw it. But his gentle nature never allowed him to give up his dream of living amongst them. Then one day, when he was working on one of those Eloi's dens, an outlaw gang rode into town and shot up the whole house— my father too. They didn't care he was just working there. They just wanted to destroy and take—like true Morlocks. But that's not the worst part. The worst part is that those Eloi, whose house my father was working, treated my father's body like it was trash. Like the Morlock he was. They packed him in a crate and mailed him back to us. No note. No nothing. Not even the payment for the work he had done. So, that's when I decided I would embrace my nature and be a Morlock. Chasing down outlaws and bringing them to justice."

"Then why you working for Honey? He's the worst of them all."

Slim looked away from Tal'dos. "He recruited me. He trained me. He gave me the gun to avenge the death of my father."

Tal'dos took a piece of folded up paper from his pocket, placed it in front of Slim, and slowly began to unfold it. When Slim read the whole thing, his eyes went wide.

"That ain't real."

"Oh, it's real," Bass came from out of the shadows and put his warrant in front of Slim.

"Pablo Honey is not only a Texas Ranger, but the leader of the Mudd-Honey gang. He was the one that shot your daddy dead in that house."

"No, I don't believe you. I don't... You're lying."

Bass leaned in and said, "Son, you know me. You know my reputation. Am I lying?"

Slim looked into Bass' eyes and knew he was telling the truth. "This is cruel irony. That father of mine."

"Which one?" Tal'dos asked sincerely.

"He was just working there, building cabinets. He never hurt nobody," Slim said, feeling something breaking inside.

"Your daddy was a good man," Bass interjected sympathetically, "didn't deserve to be gunned down like a dog in the street."

"Like a Morlock," Slim corrected him.

"Yeah, like a Morlock. But he wasn't though, was he?" Bass said.

"No, he wasn't. He was an artist."

"He deserves justice, don't you think?" Bass placed the wooden horse in Slim's breast pocket.

"Honey did that?"

"Honey didn't see your father as a man. He just saw a witness," Bass said.

Tal'dos stood up and walked over to Slim with a knife in his hand. "Now, we need your help. Are you willing?"

Slim just looked at both of them and slowly nodded his head. "What do you need from me?"

THE SHAPE OF THINGS
TO COME

It was just a shimmer in the dark, off in the distance, creating a horizon that was never there before. As it got closer, he began to see the shape of what was coming. It was a horse on fire—burning but serene. Like a Buddhist monk protesting war. But this vision didn't signal peace. It signaled something else. It was getting closer and it was heading right for him. Near this horse was his home— on fire. But no screams, just the sound of the flames licking the air—tasting its kill. And then…the horse was almost on him…and the smell of fish guts swept over him…and he heard deep within his throat… Something was forcing its way out. It was so hot. Then a cough…

"Don't give him Saki," a disembodied voice came from out of the darkness.

"It's good for him. It will help with the healing," another voice said.

Then he realized he was on the horse, but he wasn't burning.

"But he's not even conscious. You're just going to drown him."

"No, he's fine. Look, he's swallowing."

"Great, you're getting an unconscious man drunk. That will really help."

"Tal'dos, do you question your Sensei? This is an old ninja trick."

"Alright Hiro, just don't kill him."

"You have no faith in Japanese healing arts."

"Oh, I have faith in the Japanese healing arts. It's just that every healing remedy you concoct includes Saki."

"It's a very important ingredient."

"Uh huh, and I used to believe you, but then I asked Itsuko. She never heard of Saki as any ingredient for a healing remedy."

"That's because she is not ninja."

"Yeah, that is always your default answer, and because there is no other ninja here, I can never confirm that. Convenient."

Chonnie raised his right hand and said, "Ssssaki."

Tal'dos and Hiro stopped their banter and looked at Chonnie in the makeshift bed with his hand raised. "You see, it worked. He wants more," Hiro said.

Chonnie felt his mouth dry and had to struggle to lubricate his throat and mouth. "No…more…saki."

Tal'dos shot Hiro a judgmental look.

Hiro shrugged his shoulder and said, "*What?* He's awake, isn't he?"

"Where…am I? Who are you?" Chonnie had a lot of questions, but could hardly get them out. It was like he was learning to use his mouth for the first time.

"Don't try and talk too much. You are still in bad shape. We will get you some water," Tal'dos said nodding Hiro toward the direction of the water well. Hiro looked back at him in resistance. Tal'dos' eyes insisted and he pointed with his stare. Hiro reluctantly grabbed a bucket and went out to the well.

Tal'dos grabbed a rag from the side of Chonnie's bed, and wiped the side of his mouth where some of Hiro's Saki was seeping out. "My name is Tal'dos and that *there* is Hiro. When we found you, you were nearly dead. We brought you back here and patched you up. Didn't know if you were gonna make it. You were touch and go there for a while."

Hiro came back with the bucket of water. Tal'dos fished some water out with a metal cup and began to slowly pour it into Chonnie's mouth. Chonnie forced his right hand to grab the cup and began to control his own drinking. "Where am I?"

"You are here at the Kondo fishing village."

"Port Isabel?"

"South Padre actually, but yes. Can you tell us your name?"

"Yes, my name is Ascensión Ruiz de Plata," Chonnie said, in his best regal tone. No one responded, he thought. So he sighed and said, "Everyone just calls me Chonnie, though."

"Do you remember what happened to you, Chonnie?"

Just then Chonnie did. The burning horse. His father. His brother. Pablo Honey. "My father, my brother," Chonnie said

77

frantically trying to get out of bed, but his body was too weak to even sit up.

"Don't. You are still healing. You don't want to open your stitches."

"But everyone. Are they? Dead?"

Tal'dos sighed and looked into Chonnie's ojos verdes and told him everything. Even as he heard the story, he already knew. He didn't know how, but he knew. The only question he had was, "Is Inez? Is she…?"

"No," came a booming voice from the doorway, carrying a sack of supplies, "she wasn't there when it happened. She's still alive and her son, too."

Chonnie looked at the tall dark man in the doorway and immediately recognized him, "Bass Reeves."

"Yup. That's me," Bass said, setting the sack down on the table next to the fish gutting station.

"I read about you in school. You are a legend."

"Maybe once upon a time. But now…"

Just then, Chonnie realized something. He tried once again to get up and said, "We have to get to them. They are in danger. He said he would kill all of them. He has too or else…"

"…or else what?" Tal'dos asked.

"Or else they can't get the rancho," Bass answered for Chonnie.

"Yeah, they get everything. But if I get there, I can claim it for Inez and Bennie…"

Tal'dos pushed Chonnie back down again, "Hold your

horses there, Chonnie. You can't do that."

"What? Why not? Once they see I'm alive. They won't be able to…"

"They'll just kill you, again," Tal'dos said trying to calm him down. "Besides, they think you're dead. That's an advantage."

"An advantage? What do you mean?"

"The element of surprise is a formidable weapon. What they don't know can kill them?" said the small Japanese man wearing what seemed to Chonnie as a long flowing black robe with matching flowing pants and chanclas.

"Why do we need the element of surprise? If we go to the sheriff, we can have them arrested."

Bass pulled a paper from his vest pocket and handed it Chonnie. "He already has a warrant on him. Murder, robbery, and Rape."

"Well then, let's go get him."

"It's not that simple," Bass said, taking the warrant back.

Chonnie was confused, "I don't understand. Why not?"

"Because he's a Texas Ranger," Tal'dos answered.

"We can't legally touch him unless the governor allows it, and he hasn't yet. He's protected," Bass finished Tal'dos' explanation.

"So, what do we do then?" Chonnie asked sounding desperate.

"We got to kidnap him and get him to Oklahoma territory," Bass answered.

"Or we kill him," Tal'dos said angrily.

Chonnie looked at Tal'dos. He recognized the same blood lust in his eyes, "I say we kill him."

Bass stepped in, "Hold on, we can't just kill a man."

"You've killed fourteen. What's one more?" Tal'dos shot back at Bass.

"Yes, I have, but that was in self-defense. What you are talking about here is cold-blooded murder. You would be no better than him," Bass pleaded with them.

Chonnie looked at Bass and sat up for the first time without feeling the pain in his chest, "I don't want to be better. I want him dead for what he did to my family—my home."

"I understand you're hurting, son. But this ain't the way. We can bring him in and he can face justice."

"Justice. Such an abstract concept to me right now. It's high minded morals. When I was studying law, I believed that justice was sending criminals to jail. Getting some sense of peace for the victims. I thought that was the better path—the right path. But then that rinche blew my brother's face off right in front of me. And you know, something happened. I realized justice is sometimes answered in bullets not bars," Chonnie felt the anger fill him.

"That's the pain talking. Killing ain't so simple a thing. It sticks with you. No matter how much in the right you think you are," Bass answered Chonnie, trying to deter him.

"I say we take a vote," Tal'dos said, breaking the tension between the two of them. "I vote for killing him."

"Kill him," Chonnie said still with a locked gaze on Bass.

"Me too," Hiro said from behind them.

"This ain't no democracy. This is the law. You kill him, I will have to chase you down for murder."

"The votes are three to one. We're doing this," Chonnie said, looking at Tal'dos. "What do we have to do?"

"Is this the shape of things to come?" Bass asked the room.

"Bass, you knew when you came along this was the end-game," Tal'dos turned to Bass and touched his shoulder. "For Mape'l. For Running Coyote. For Chonnie's family. For all of the pain and destruction Honey has caused."

"You know there is an old saying. When you go looking for vengeance..."

"...dig two graves," Hiro finished.

"Well, I'm already dead. I might as well have the vengeance too," Chonnie said.

"Are you in, old friend?" Tal'dos said softly to Bass. "We can't do this without you."

"Fine, I'll help you plan, but I aim to capture first," Bass set down his foot.

"Okay. That's fine—because Honey ain't gonna let us just take him in."

"What do we do first?" Chonnie asked.

"First," Hiro said to Chonnie, "You train."

SINCE YOU BEEN GONE

Here's the thing. It wasn't that she didn't want to visit them. It wasn't that at all. The last six months had been the most trying. Trying to figure the ins and outs of ranching. Trying to deal with vaqueros leaving. Being shorthanded. The lynchings were becoming more frequent. As were the whispers, that she couldn't do this, growing louder than chicharras in the night. She even had to start letting renters on the rancho—Anglos. It was all slipping from her fingers, and she couldn't catch her breath. So, when she received the message that the headstones were ready, Inez saddled up Güero, Chonnie's horse. She rode out on her own in disguise. With a workman's shirt, pants, and a vaquero's hat. Her trusty shotgun holstered in her saddle. and Macario's .45 tucked in her belt. She knew it was dangerous. But she had to come out on this day. To see them—the gravestones. embossed with flowers and silver coins. Like their namesake.

The graveyard was ten miles at the end of the rancho on the Puente-Plata line. It was fenced off with wrought iron and a large plaque that simply read, Plata. When she arrived, it was still early. The dew was still hanging on the world like eye crusties waiting for the sun to rub them out. Inez walked up to see the two largest stones, shiny and new. They were for Daniel and Herlinda. To the right of Daniel's was Macario's stone. Inez felt the lump in her throat. To the left of Herlinda was Chonnie's, looking so small compared to the rest. Even tía Carmen's seemed bigger. But Chonnie's was the one that caused her dam of composure to break. The tears streamed down her face.

With the back of her hand, she wiped the tears from her cheeks. "I'm sorry I haven't been here since…since…it happened…I just couldn't. It's been so hard since you been gone." Inez moved to Macario's grave and slowly began to feel the lettering. "Bennie, he misses you so much. He's leaving for school, though. He leaves in a week. I don't know how I will keep going without him here. I…I…I know he has to go. He can't be here. Things are getting worse. Los diablos de rinches are getting worse. They are killing more and more of the men. I don't know what to do." She cried. It was like a release she had never felt before. Everything spilled out of her.

Inez sat down between Herlinda and Chonnie. She stared out at the range. She leaned against Chonnie's gravestone. "It seems so long ago now—when we would come out here and leave pan dulce for the dead on Día de los muertos. Now, it will be for you." The stone was so cold, but somehow it was comforting. "You weren't even back for a day before…and the last thing I said was… so cruel. I wish I could take it all back. I wish I had told you I loved you. But you broke my heart, Ascensión Ruiz de Plata. You broke it into a thousand little pieces." A last lonely tear tumbled out of the side of her eye. She wiped it from her face. Then, for a second, she saw something sticking out of the dirt on Chonnie's grave. She blinked and looked even harder. She leaned in closer and saw a tiny hand sticking out of the ground. She reached over and felt it. Yes, it was real. She grabbed it between her fingers and pulled. It didn't provide too much resistance. Out of the ground came this small figurine with a painted face and no shirt.

"Zartan!" Inez heard herself say, and then she looked around and smiled. Inez stood up and looked around, holding Zartan tight. There was nothing, and no one on the horizon. But it was a sign that he was still with her. Chonnie was still with her. From the pit of despair, Inez climbed out of herself. For the first time in months, she felt like she wasn't alone. Chonnie had sent this to her from the other side. It was more than ghostly. It was hope. She wiped her face, kissed each of the gravestones, and mounted her horse. Zartan tucked into her breast pocket. And rode off back home.

"What are you doing?" Tal'dos said, startling Chonnie who laid prone to the ground with a pair of binoculars, covered in grass and dirt.

"Jesus, you scared me," Chonnie said, never tearing his eyes from the spy glass.

"Have you been sneaking up here? Dodging your training? It's only been two months. You aren't ready for this." Tal'dos said, sounding like his mother when she caught him messing about.

"Don't be silly. I've been watching her."

"You know how seriously creepy that sounds, right?"

Chonnie put the binoculars down and looked up at Tal'dos, "I just wanted to make sure she was okay."

"What if someone saw you? You could have blown our entire operation," Tal'dos shook his head.

"I've kept my distance. I've been using Hiro's techniques. No one saw me."

"And the toy?"

"What? How did you know that?"

"They don't call me the Long Eye for nothing."

"Look, she's been in such bad shape. I just wanted to give her a little something—some hope."

"Really? I think you want to tell her you're still alive. You can't. You know that. No one can know."

Chonnie sat up and brushed off the grassy camouflage and said, "I know. It's just…"

"You have to be strong," Tal'dos said, realizing how hard this was for Chonnie. "Look, I know this is difficult. But when this is done, you can have your life back," Tal'dos lied. He knew there was no going back. That life was gone. But like Chonnie did for Inez, Tal'dos knew he needed hope.

"Besides, you're not the only one watching her. We have someone watching over her."

Chonnie perked up a little. "Really, who?"

"Tsisdu's."

"Rabbits? Really."

"I have rapport with all of the creatures of this land. It's an

Indian thing."

"Come on. I'm not ten," Chonnie said, as Tal'dos helped him to his feet.

"It's true. Sometimes you just have to listen to the wind. It carries all the songs of the world. I know how to listen. You will have to work on that. I can teach you."

Chonnie, finally on his feet, brushed off the last of the dirt and started to walk back with Tal'dos. "Really, you are going to teach me to listen to the wind and somehow get messages from the rabbits?"

"Birds too. They never shut up. Anyway, there has been a development since you been gone."

"Really, what?"

"Let's get back to the village. It's better if we all hear this together."

THE INTIMIDATION GAME

Today was the day. The day it was all supposed to be over. The Plata rancho was supposed to be sold, lock, stock, and barrel to the Kings. Today was the day she was supposed to sign. Stillwell waited in his office on this hot September morning. She was late. Thirty minutes to be exact. Stillwell looked down at the sale papers on his desk for the tenth time. Fifty dollars an acre for one hundred acres. Plus, ten thousand for the hacienda, and ten dollars a head for their cattle. It was a generous deal considering the alternative, Stillwell thought.

The bell over the door shook and rang out. It was Inez Plata with an older Mexican man he had never met. He was dressed in a brown suit. Inez was dressed like a vaquero down to the boots and hat, and a .45 holstered to her hip. She also carried an old beat up shotgun. Inez walked right up to Stillwell's desk and said, "Mr. Stillwell. We are here."

"Well, señora Plata. I'm glad you are here. Have a seat. And who is this?" Stillwell asked feeling that something was off.

"This is señor Tomás Acosta. He is my lawyer," Inez

answered, taking a seat and setting the shotgun down against the desk.

"Señora Plata, that is not necessary. Everything here is on the up and up," Stillwell said, sounding weaselly.

Acosta began the conversation, "Mr. Stillwell, I am only here to make sure that señora Plata and her son get a fair shake out of this deal. This is a big decision."

"Of course, I completely understand," Stillwell said smiling, but cringing on the inside.

"Can I see the deal, please?" Inez asked.

"Here it is. All worked out," Stillwell said, handing her the document.

Inez looked at it. She quickly got lost in all the technical terms and small print. She looked over at Tomás and handed him the paper. "Fifty dollars an acre seems a little low, no?" Inez asked.

"Señora Plata, that is a fair price for a failing rancho like yours. Mr. Kleberg is being very generous for rescuing you from all of the debt you have accumulated over the last few months."

Inez exchanged glances with Tomás as he looked over the document, and then she said, "That is only because several of my vaqueros have been murdered—my cattle poisoned. If I didn't know any better, I would think you and your employers are trying to push me off my land."

"Clients," Stillwell corrected.

"What?" Inez responded.

"Clients. The King family—John Kleberg to be exact. He is my client, not my employer. I am a lawyer. I am my own employer."

"Really?" Inez said, as she laid the shotgun across her lap. "With the way your *clients* are buying up Mexican Tejano ranchos, it seems like highway robbery. These ranchos have been in these family's hands for hundreds of years, and now with the rinches…"

"Señora, the *Texas Rangers* are here to protect all of us from the increasing amount of bandidos that have been raiding from across the border. It is not Mr. Kleberg's fault that the Mexicans can't control their criminals," Stillwell said with a more forceful tone.

"Mr. Stillwell," Tomás interrupted, "this document says that the Platas give up everything for only a total of twenty thousand dollars. That seems a little low, don't you think?"

Stillwell turned to Tomás Acosta and said, "Señor Acosta, are you trying to negotiate here?"

"I think that a minimum of seventy-five would be more appropriate," Tomás challenged Stillwell.

"Seventy-five? No one gets seventy-five. Not in this day and age. The railroad has changed everything. Ranching is a dying industry here. Agriculture—*that* is the future. If you want to ranch, go to West Texas, or better yet, back to Mexico. That is where you would be *better* appreciated," Stillwell started to feel his temper rising from his gut.

"Mr. Stillwell," Inez brought his attention back to her, "It's funny you talk about agriculture. Citrus, cotton, sugarcane. All these things require some sort of irrigation, right?"

"Well, look who's studied up on the science of agriculture."

"I don't know if you are insulting me because I am Mexican

Tejana or a woman, but I would remind you, Mr. Stillwell, that I am the *patrona* of the Plata rancho you are so desperately trying to buy," Inez found a strength she didn't know she had. She reached to her gun belt, and in the crease between her shirt and the belt, she felt for Zartan. She kept him there ever since the graveyard. She had heard of the intimidation game that the Anglos play, but this was the first time she had been the target of it.

Stillwell realized that anger was not a useful tactic here. She did not scare easily for such a young woman. "You are right, señora Plata. Irrigation is needed."

"Then I would say that I would like to amend the contract you have proposed here today. I am fine with the amounts for the land and the cattle and even the hacienda, but…"

"…but what?" Stillwell interrupted her.

"I want fifty thousand for the water rights."

"Fifty thousand?" Stillwell knew that something was definitely off here. How could she know that the water was what he was really after?

"Yes, fifty thousand. You see, my uncle has worked as a sugarcane farmer for years down around Hidalgo. He told me that there had been several Anglos asking about irrigation. They are trying to create a huge irrigation system from Rio Grande City to Brownsville. And with the railroad, that would mean millions for those who own those massive farms. Because they could ship that produce all around the country and into Mexico too. So, I think that fifty thousand is a fair amount. Don't you, Mr. Stillwell?"

"Well, señora, I see you have your finger on the pulse of the future. But what you fail to see in this negotiation tactic of yours, is that you must be holding an ace to play this gamble, and you don't have it. You are seriously in debt and you don't have the men to stop these bandidos from raiding your stock. You can't protect your precious hacienda from terrible things happening. Not even Daniel Plata had that kind of protection, and he had many more men than you do right now. But I am a fair man and I will amend the document to include the water rights for ten thousand dollars."

"And if I don't sell?" Inez countered.

Stillwell leaned back in his big leather chair and said, "I don't advise that, señora Plata. That is not a fight you wish to start. We don't want to see you or your son—Bennie is it?—getting hurt, or worse."

"Are you threatening me, Mr. Stillwell?" Inez squeezed Zartan's head.

"I'm just stating the facts that it is a dangerous time with all these bandidos running around. You never know what could happen, and without the help of the Rangers—I don't know how you would fare out there on that rancho all alone."

Inez was furious. She so badly wanted to pull out her .45 and shoot him between the eyes, but she knew she couldn't. Instead she stood up and said, "Mr. Stillwell, I am not selling. Not with these numbers. And I will be ready—for any *bandidos* that come my way. Good day, sir." Inez gestured for Tomás to get up and leave. Tomás got up and placed the contract back on the desk. He tipped his hat to Stillwell. Inez turned and stormed out of his office. Acosta trailing after her.

On the street, Inez felt her hands shaking from fear and anger rolled into one.

"Do you think it is wise to challenge Stillwell in your present state?" Tomás Acosta asked her.

"I don't care. I just started a war. I need to get Bennie out of here now."

"Señora Plata, you are going to need a miracle," he said, and then after a long pause continued, "I don't mean to be insensitive, but do you have the money you promised."

Inez looked at him and pulled a rolled-up wad of bills from her pocket and handed it to him. That money was almost the last of the Plata riches, "Thank you, Tomás. You have done enough."

Inez and Tomás parted ways, and Inez walked back to the cart where Adán and Ernesto were waiting to take her back to the rancho. "Adán, Ernesto, we need men. Where can we get them?"

"That is going to be difficult. They are all afraid of the rinches, but I will go to Mexico and see what we can get," Adán said, as he whipped the horses into trotting.

Back in the office, Stillwell sat there feeling completely blindsided. "She's going to be trouble," Honey said, entering from his back entrance.

"I didn't think she had it in her. A week ago, she was nearly broken. Something changed."

"That girl has bigger huevos than you, that's for sure."

"We are going to have to stop her before she rallies the other families," Stillwell said scheming.

"We can take her at the rancho."

"No, she'll be expecting that. I have a better idea. Her boy, Bennie, is going up to San Antonio in two days. He is going by train," Stillwell said, smiling at Honey.

"And trains are always getting robbed by bandidos," Honey finished his thought.

"Get it done. Both of 'em. Leave no Plata alive."

"You got it, boss," Honey said smiling. He had been itchin' for some killing. And a good old fashion train robbery was just what the doctor ordered.

A RUSH OF BLOOD
TO THE HEAD

The camera lens is the purest, coldest eye. It sees with no judgement. No doubt. Just focus. Snap. The shutter clicks shut. Freezes the moment forever, then moves on to the next shot. This is what Chonnie had running through his mind as he leveled his Colt at the heart of the rinche. It was what Bass had taught him when aiming at paper targets on trees. Just do. Don't think. It will cause you to hesitate. And that second is everything—life and death. A weight so heavy it will crush you if you let it.

"You have to be colder than ice if your gonna kill a man before he gets you. Because, believe me, he will have no compunction about killing you," Bass had told him before he embarked on this crazy mission.

Breathe, just breathe, and pull that trigger, Chonnie told himself as he pulled the trigger and—BLAM!

"I just got word that Honey is planning to hit the train heading to San Antonio in two days," Tal'dos explained to Chonnie, Bass, and Hiro standing around a large round table that was once a railroad spool for wire.

"Two days. That's…Inez and Bennie's train," Chonnie said, feeling the moisture drain from his mouth.

"Yes, I know. They are planning to assassinate them and make it look like bandidos hit the train. They are to look like collateral damage," Tal'dos explained.

"How do you know this?" Chonnie asked, suspicious of Tal'dos' intel.

"I told you I have spies everywhere."

"Rabbits told you Honey's entire plan?" Chonnie asked skeptically.

Bass stepped up and said, "We got a man inside, Chonnie."

"What are we going to do?" Chonnie asked, sounding desperate. "We have to stop them."

Hiro stepped up and said, "Chonnie, you are not ready."

"Hiro, you are the one that's been telling me that the best way to test my skills is by actually being in the fight. Well, this is my chance."

"You haven't embraced the shadows. The way of the ninja depends on shadow. This will go down in broad daylight. YOU are not ready for that," Hiro pleaded with Chonnie.

"But I *am* ready for this," Chonnie said, pulling his .45 from his holster. "I'm a crack shot. I always have been. Bass can confirm that."

"You may be a crack shot with paper targets, but it's different when the bullets start flying," Bass interjected.

"We don't have a choice," Tal'dos broke into their argument, "They will kill them both if we don't stop them. And if Honey is there, we can put an end to this once and for all."

"What's their plan? They can't just ride up with their rinche badges and shoot them dead," Chonnie asked.

"No, the plan is that Honey and Blind Tommy will be riding the train. The rest of them will ride up like bandidos and start shooting up the train. Honey and Blind Tommy will make it look like they are stopping them. But in the shootout, Inez and Bennie are to be killed. That's the plan," Tal'dos said, pulling a folded-up map from his pocket. He laid it flat on the table. It was a South Texas railroad map from Brownsville to Austin.

"I say we ride up there like bandidos ourselves and stop them," Chonnie offered as a plan.

"I don't know about this. Too much could go wrong," Bass said, studying the map.

"We would need a man on the inside to make sure Honey or Blind Tommy don't shoot Inez and Bennie," Bass said.

Tal'dos looked hard at Bass. Bass looked up and grunted.

"Who better than the famous Bass Reeves to give Honey and Tommy pause," Tal'dos said smiling.

"Great, then Tal'dos and I will be the bandidos. How many men are going to be riding up on the train?" Chonnie asked.

"Three, but one is our man. He will be wearing a yellow bandana. Don't shoot him," said Tal'dos.

Hiro stood in the background. He had a gold pocket watch in his hand that had a deep dent on the cover. He fingered the dent excitedly because he could feel a rush of blood to his head. It was that same rush when he planned missions. When he was young and ninja. But now, with a bum leg and arthritis surging through his fingers, he knew he couldn't be in the action. He was too old, too broken, too thirsty.

"Hiro?" Tal'dos said, rousing him from his reverie, "Are you with us?"

"I am always with you, Tal'dos. But my body is another story. It betrays me at every step. I don't think I would be an asset on this mission," Hiro admitted, feeling that rush of blood subside.

"We just need you to do one thing," Tal'dos said.

"What is that?" Hiro asked suspiciously.

Tal'dos smiled, "We need you to go birdwatching."

Chonnie felt the rush of blood to his head as he practiced shooting at Bass' old wanted posters. He felt the rush like nothing else in his life. They were finally going to do something. He might even have his chance to kill Pablo Honey for what he did to his family. With every shot he fired, he pictured Honey's smug face as he pulled the trigger that ended his brother's life.

"You better check that vengeance. That rush of blood to your head that you are feeling ain't gonna be the same out there," Bass said from over Chonnie's shoulder. He had been watching him for an hour now.

"I can do this, Bass. I need to do this," Chonnie said,

reloading his six shooter.

"You know—you might not make it out of this alive."

"I'm not afraid to die, Bass."

"I know you ain't. But it's not just you out there. You're part of a team, and you have to watch your partner's backs. You can't let killing Honey overshadow your commitment to your partners. Besides, what about that woman you are in love with and her kid? They'll be in the crossfire."

"I'm not in love with her. She's my brother's wife."

"She was. She's not anymore. But that's not the point."

"What's the point, Bass?" Chonnie said starting to get angry.

"The point is, bloodlust has a funny way of blinding you to the bigger picture."

"What's the bigger picture?"

"This is a rescue mission, not an assassination. If you go in there just wanting to kill, you might get some good people hurt or worse."

"Tal'dos is in this to kill Honey too. Did you have this talk with him?"

"Tal'dos is trained. He's been in fights. He knows his priorities. You, son, I don't know about yet."

"I'll be fine, Bass."

"I hope so. Because what's coming tomorrow—those deeds stick with you forever. And that rush you feelin' won't help you. Not like you think. You got to be cold—like a camera."

BANDIDOS!

Blind Tommy Melon wasn't blind—not really. He just had poor eyesight. He couldn't focus on things more than eight feet from his face. That's why he preferred the street sweeper. It took care of business, scattering pellets everywhere. Very little aiming involved. For many bosses in this line of work, that would be a problem. But not for Pablo Honey. He took him in back when they were with the Mudd-Honey gang. He saw something in Tommy that no one ever had. It was unwavering loyalty and a willingness to do what it took to get the job done without questions. The other guys, August Beall and Norman Faulk, always thought themselves better than Tommy. They're the ones that gave him the nickname Blind Tommy. He hated it at first, but then Pablo told him, *the only way to fight back against teasing like that is by embracing the name. Make it your own. Besides, it's kind of scary seeing a man named Blind Tommy welding a street sweeper in their direction. It keeps 'em guessing.*

Slim, on the other hand, never picked on Blind Tommy. He was his best friend ever since they picked him up in Denton. They had taken to each other because they were both different than the other guys. Slim liked to carve all sorts of things with his knife, and Blind Tommy was, well, blind. But on this day, Pablo chose him to be his wing man on this all-important mission. They were there to kill a woman and her kid. The other guys might object to that, but not Blind Tommy. He was bent on impressing Pablo. He would do anything, and this was it. The other guys were the "bandidos" coming to rob the train. They were supposed to aim high and miss, which was easy for Tommy. He couldn't use a pistol to save his life.

The 9:15 train to San Antonio was full. Pablo and Blind Tommy wore their badges prominently on their lapels. Their guns in their hip holsters. They sat two rows behind the woman and her kid. Tommy had gotten a good look at her when they boarded the train. *She was a looker for a Mexican*, Blind Tommy thought. She had long jet-black hair, Indian-like. Brown skin, but not too brown. *It must be the sun that baked her this color*, he thought. And green eyes like he had never seen on a Mexican. The boy had them too. She was small, but he could see a fierceness in her eyes. He liked that. Blind Tommy fingered the trigger on his gun and licked his lips. He quickly glanced at Pablo to make sure he hadn't seen. He hadn't, so he turned his attention to the window and the train station bustling with people. Pablo was reading a newspaper. He paid no attention to anything Blind Tommy was doing.

"Howdy, may I take this seat?" a deep booming voice asked.

Pablo pushed his newspaper down to see a tall older looking black man in black hat, black vest and a federal marshal badge on his chest. He didn't like this, but he had no choice, "Sure, why not?"

"Thank you kindly. I see you all are brothers in blue, too."

"We're law enforcement, yes. But I don't think we are brothers," Pablo said with distain in his tone.

"Different outfits?"

"Texas Rangers," Pablo answered.

"Ahh, Rangers, state coppers."

"Yep, and you sir?"

"Name's Bass Reeves, U.S. Federal Marshal for the Muskogee district of Southern Oklahoma and North Texas. Currently out of Paris."

"Paris? France?"

"Funny, you're the second fellow to make that same mistake. No, Paris, Texas."

"Huh," Pablo Honey sighed now knowing who he was, "So, you're the marshal that arrested my man awhile back."

"Your man was a Walter Waterson, right? Goes by Slim."

"That'd be him. I caught him for trespassing. Didn't know who he was until I got him back to the jail in Brownsville and we had to send word to Austin."

"Tell me, what's a federal marshal doing down in this neck of the woods? You ain't got no jurisdiction here."

"I have special business here."

"Next time, you might want to believe a man when he tells you he's a Ranger. It might save you plenty of hassle."

"True that. But he wasn't wearing no badge, like you two boys."

Pablo just smiled and nodded his head. The conversation was over. He put the newspaper back in front of his face. Bass just leaned back in his seat and tipped his hat forward to cover his eyes.

Tommy looked from Pablo, who was clearly angry, to Bass, who was clearly smirking. He knew there was something going on there. He didn't do anything because Pablo never signaled him. He cast his gaze back to the moving scenery and knew that when the time came, the coon marshal was dead.

Hiro stood at the top of the hill. His hips were hurting from riding that damn horse all night. He was set up about an hour north of the Brownsville station. It was mostly ranch land—and it was hot. Hiro was thirsty too, but Tal'dos had hidden his Saki. He was much better than Itsuko at hiding things. And he was also a little hurt because he was the lookout on this mission. That was rookie work, and he was no rookie. But he couldn't fight anymore. So here he was, with a long spyglass and Tal'dos' hair brushing mirror.

After about an hour, Bass pushed his hat back up his head and positioned it comfortably. Pablo Honey had finished his paper by then and was just looking out at the moving landscape.

"You know, Ranger, you never asked me about my special business."

Pablo looked back at Bass, startled that he was talking to him again. "I figured it ain't my business. We got our own to worry about."

"Well, Mr. Honey. This might concern you dearly."

Pablo was shocked. He knew his name. "Oh really," is all he said though.

"Yeah. See, I had this partner. His name was Running Coyote. Worked with him for over twenty years up in the Oklahoma territory. He was one of the finest I ever worked with, but he had problems. You know, like men do. He liked the drink and he liked to gamble. It was those things that led him to neglect his family and squander his earnings. But at heart, he was a good man. Just couldn't stop himself, you know—like a sickness eating at him. He turned to some pretty unscrupulous fellows to borrow money. He had a line on a fight—prize fight. He heard that the fix was in on that fight. It was a sure bet, he was told. So, he borrowed big. And when all was said and done, that fight *was* fixed. Just not the way he bet. He had been lied to, and now he owed way too much to the wrong people. Do you know what happened to him?"

"Someone came along to collect, I'm guessing," Pablo answered knowing this story sounded familiar.

"Yeah, someone did. But not from Running Coyote. No, these jackals—they took it out on his wife and child. Did bad things to his wife and made the child watch. Then someone shot her in the chest with a Dragoon. Like that cannon you got on you. The child escaped though. Running Coyote never found his child. He looked the rest of his life, but he never found anything. I got that case, but we never had a suspect. Not until last year, when ol' Running Coyote lay on his deathbed. He told me he knew exactly who did it. But he never said because he owed them so much money. So, he covered it up. But right before he died, he gave me the name of that moneylender. I paid that moneylender a visit, and I got that name out of him. The name of the man who carried out that hit. You want to know the name of that man?"

Pablo already had his hand on his pistol, gripped tight. Bass just pulled back his jacket and revealed a folded-up paper in his shirt pocket. Bass slowly pulled it from his pocket and unfolded it. "That name," Bass finally said, facing the warrant at Pablo, "is Pablo Honey."

"You know, I'm a lieutenant in the Texas Rangers and *that* warrant can't be served without the governor's expressed permission."

"I know that. Where do you think I'm heading?"

Pablo smiled and removed his hand from his gun, "Good luck with that."

It was about 10:30 when Hiro heard the whistle blow, and then he saw three men riding in from the brush. They had bandanas over their faces. Two black and one yellow. That's what he had been waiting for. Hiro flashed the mirror down the hill toward Chonnie and Tal'dos, who were waiting in the brush for Hiro's signal. They were dressed like Mexican bandidos but with special ninja masks over their faces. These masks were unique because they covered the entire face, except the eyes. They were also made from a special material that quieted breathing. But that was useless on this mission. Hiro flashed the light three times, and they sprung to action.

"That badge might protect you now, but I always get my

man," Bass promised.

"That may be, but this is Texas. Things work different here. I would be more worried about what it would look like for a black boy like you trying to arrest a white man. Let's see who swings from a rope then. If I was a bettin' man, I would bet on white. Black ain't particularly lucky around here. We got something special for uppity coons like you…"

Just then, a gunshot went through the window, cutting off their intimidation game—forcing all three of them to pull their guns. They had no choice but to point them outside.

Three men with bandanas on their faces were riding hard against the train, firing every which way. Pablo thought about pointing his gun at Bass and being done with it, but there were too many witnesses. He needed to stick to the plan, at least for now. Both Blind Tommy and Pablo returned fire wide. Bass also took aim, but he missed when Blind Tommy crashed into him. "Sorry about that," was all he said.

Bass knew this was going to be tricky. He also knew that he had to protect Inez and Bennie. Everything else had to wait.

Chonnie had never ridden a horse this hard in his life. It felt like they were almost airborne. The wind rushing past his face. Chonnie leveled his pistol at the back of one of the black bandanas and fired. The shot went wide through a window. The shot caused one of the black bandanas to turn back and fire. That shot went wide too. The element of surprise was up. Tal'dos came up and fired a shot that seemed to clip the black bandana, but it didn't stop him. It just caused him to ride lower on his horse and fire back at them.

Tal'dos fired at the yellow bandana but clearly missed on purpose. The yellow bandana returned the same false aimed shot back at Tal'dos.

Chonnie saw a black bandana get up alongside the train and jump on the back of one of the passenger cars. Chonnie knew he had to get him before he got inside, so he rode hard at the train. He came up alongside where the black bandana had jumped on the car. Everything was moving so fast. But he saw the handle bar he had to grab, and focused on it hard. He remembered what Hiro had taught him about breathing. He took three deep breaths to steady himself and leapt off his horse. He caught the bar, but he didn't have any footing. So he swung around a few times from the rush of the train and managed to pull himself up. In the process, he dropped his gun. Luckily, he was carrying two extra like Bass told him. One on the hip, and one in the small of the back.

Chonnie finally got up on the platform and looked through the window into the passenger car. Just then, a bullet shattered the glass causing him to cover his face and fall backward. He lost his hat to the rushing wind but managed not to fall off the train. He grabbed the pistol on his hip and slid up against the door. His back to the door. He peeked inside. Another shot. It was the black bandana firing. He took a deep breath again and recited to himself, "Be like a camera. Be like a camera." He waited for the report of black bandana's gun and then turned. He pointed his gun dead center on black bandana's chest and fired. Black bandana flew back, crashing into some of the passengers. They were all screaming. A bullet whizzed by his head, and he saw Tal'dos' black bandana shooting at him. Before Chonnie could react, the Black bandana's eye exploded from his head and he fell off his horse. Tal'dos was behind him with his Winchester. He nodded at Chonnie and Chonnie nodded back.

Pablo Honey was livid. Two of his men were dead, and now he couldn't even shoot the girl and her boy. His cover story was blown. All he could do was shoot at the two other bandidos and watch them ride away. They were chasing Slim. He knew that Slim would give them the slip. But still, this was more than coincidence. This marshal. The other bandidos. It was all connected somehow. He didn't know how, but he aimed to find out. Bass shots went wide too. It seemed like Bass was just as intent on not killing them as he was. He had to let it go and consider this a failed plan.

The San Antonio Express News, on the other hand, didn't let it go. They splashed Pablo and Blind Tommy's faces all over the papers, commending them for foiling an attempted train robbery. Bass was nowhere to be seen though. The only note in the stories was that a federal marshal aided the Texas Rangers in this firefight. No name—just a federal marshal.

PART II

THE DARK SIDE OF THE MOON

Hang on. Just hang on, said the moon to the victims of the night. But they couldn't hear—not tonight. Not while the dark side of the moon shone. Not even the stars bothered to come out on this night. They couldn't stomach to light this night. They couldn't bear to witness. No snap came when their feet dangled in the air because the rope was too slack. Its only job was to choke. And choke it did. If only it would have been tighter. That would have been mercy. It creaked with the weight of what it held. And as they swung, the moon wept the day into being, leaving behind a fog that blanketed this nightmare that only men could fathom. It was such a horrid thing that even the flies and the vultures stayed away—for at least the break of dawn. But dawn is relentless in revealing everything.

On that morning a witness would emerge. A witness that would hear the moon weep. He rode in on a grey horse and carried with him a secret that had nothing to do with what had happened the night before. He was traveling the trail as he did every dawn. But this dawn held special meaning for the witness. He wanted to see the fruit of his labor. To see the woman that still held his heart—that he swore saw his eyes in the heat of battle. *And maybe,* he thought, *she recognized me.* It was only a split second. Right after he shot the black bandana. He looked right at her frightened face. That is when he was sure she knew. But the smoke snatched that moment from him. That dawn made the weight of the world feel a little lighter. That dawn brought for him a new sense of joy that he had not felt in a long time. But like all moments of joy in a tragedy, they are fleeting. And when the rider became witness to what the dark side of the moon brought, all joy fled him. Because in that agonizing morning, all he could be was a witness.

The witness dismounted his grey horse. He gazed upon a nightmare like he had never seen. It was a family that he knew. It was the Suarez's—Ignacio, Petra, and their two daughters, Alicia and Judy. They all swung in the wind like some hellish swing set. Ignacio had his pants around his ankles. There was nothing left between his legs except blood blackened by time. His face purple from the rope around his neck. Petra was almost unrecognizable. Her blouse torn open. Breasts exposed to the world. A dark stain on the front of her skirt and in the back. But the worst was her face. Her nose was just a gaping hole of clotted blood and a substance the witness couldn't even begin to recognize. The monsters who did this seemed to hesitate when it came to the two girls, who were no more than seven and five. They seemed untouched, but purple faced from the noose. Then he saw it—the thing that caused the witness to fall to his knees. On the backside of Alicia was a note nailed into her that read: *You take 2 of ours.* On the backside of

Judy was the second half of the note. It read: *We take 4 of yours.*

In that moment, the rider went from witness to guilty party. He left all his breakfast on the ground. It was the only penance his body could give at that moment. He knew that this was because of what they had done. And for the first time since this crazy mission started, he understood what Bass had been trying to tell him about the bigger picture. There were always consequences. Bass tried to drill this into Chonnie on the morning they left to stop Pablo Honey. Chonnie couldn't hear him. Now, it was all he could think about. "I did this," Chonnie muttered under his breath as he wiped away the spittle from his mouth.

"No, señor, we didn't do nothing," a woman's voice pierced the morning air. It was off in the distance. Chonnie didn't hesitate. He got to his feet and ran toward the sound. Something in him had broken out. It was something he never felt. It was cold and calm.

Chonnie kept as quiet as the ground like Hiro had taught him. He crept up to the scene in question. It was the Garcias— Nestor and Gloria. They were the Plata's most loyal servants. Gloria was their cook and Chonnie's nursemaid. Nestor took care of the grounds. All its creaks and leaks. All its problems. He would patch it up. The Garcia's were on the hacienda supply cart. They seemed to be stopped by two Texas Rangers on horseback. He didn't recognize them, but one of them had a shotgun across his lap. The other was obviously in charge. He was the only one that spoke.

"I see you got hogs there that don't seem to belong to you," the leader said.

"Señor, they come from the Plata rancho. We were just

going to town to sell," Gloria did all the talking because Nestor didn't speak English.

"You two don't look well off enough to own the Plata rancho," the leader pressed them.

"We work for señora Plata. We are not criminals," Gloria pleaded with the leader.

"It don't matter, anyhow, the only good Mexican is…" the leader didn't have a chance to finish. A masked figure came out of nowhere. Knocked his partner from his horse, while at the same time wrapping his legs around the leader's neck, pulling him to the ground. The Ranger with the shotgun was instantly knocked unconscious, but the leader was still conscious. He was seeing stars and couldn't get his bearings, nonetheless awake.

"Who sent you?" Chonnie said in his best Anglo accent.

"What the hell are you?" the Ranger said befuddled by a man in a full black face mask. Only his green eyes were visible.

"I'm the witness to your sins," Chonnie said, as he socked him across the jaw and grabbed his collar. Chonnie pulled him closer, "Are you one of Honey's men?"

Confused, the Ranger answered, "Honey? No, I work for Captain Baker."

"Baker? Who's Baker?"

"He's the commander around these parts."

"Did you kill the Saurez's?"

"Who?"

"The family that was lynched down the road."

"What does it matter? You gonna kill us anyway."

"I ain't gonna kill you. I want you to tell your boss that there's a new player in town. And I aim to stop all of you. Whatever it takes."

"Baker is not going to take this lightly. You just assaulted two Texas Rangers…" Chonnie struck him across the temple which instantly knocked him out. Hiro's training finally started to pay off.

"Señor?" señora Garcia called out to him.

Chonnie hesitated to face them, in case they recognized him. "You should go now. You don't want to be here for what comes next."

"Muchas gracias, señor, but they will just come back with more men. It will be much worse."

"No, they won't," Chonnie said, "because I will protect you."

"And who are you?"

"A reckoning," and with that, Chonnie was gone. He had finally learned the art of walking in shadow on this morning. The dark side of the moon had left just enough darkness to let him slip into shadow and vanish.

STRONG ENOUGH

Is there a word for the last breath? If there isn't, there should be. Something so significant should have a name, and that in itself is a tragedy. Inez could never stop her mind when she was stressed. Today, as they laid three more of her vaqueros to rest, she could not help but think about their last breaths. What did it sound like? Was it a gurgle? Was it terrible? Was it sweet relief? It definitely needs to be named.

"Patrona? We have to go," Adán Peña said, breaking her from her thoughts. Adán carried a shotgun everywhere he went. Before the matanza of the Plata family, he was simply a driver and kept the gun empty. But now, with the rinches, he always kept it loaded. He also carried a .45 Long Colt tucked into his belt.

Inez grabbed some fresh dirt and sprinkled it on their caskets. "Sí, vámonos aquí." Inez followed Adán back to their carriage and climbed in. She wore her long flowing black dress with black bonnet. She never thought she would have to wear it so soon after the matanza of her family. But it seemed that nowadays, it was seeing plenty of wear.

When the train to San Antonio was attacked, she was sure they were there to kill her and her son. But the bandidos were killed by some strange masked man. There was something about his eyes. There was a comfort there. She couldn't quite understand, but she knew she was safe now. The lynching of the Suarez's was the worst of the attacks. She didn't know if she was strong enough to keep fighting the rinches. As the carriage pulled away, she reached into the cleavage of her dress and rubbed the head of Zartan she had tucked next to her left breast. It gave her strength when she didn't think she had any. On this day, this day of mourning for three men that had served the Plata's for years, it was a comfort she needed. The rinches weren't going to stop until they had her land, and she didn't know what to do.

The Plata hacienda looked more like a fort now than the home of a loving family. The hacienda's gates were always closed, and two men stood guard at all times. There was barbed wire on the wall that surrounded the house. It reminded Inez of a prison and in many ways, it was. For as long as Inez could remember, the hacienda had an air of welcome to it. Now, it screamed stay out. Oh, how times have changed. The dangers were so close to their doorstep that she hardly slept. Hope was fading fast, and poor Zartan's head was being whittled away from the constant rubbing. But then, like things do, the winds changed.

As Adán pulled the carriage up the gate of the hacienda, Inez saw two large furry eyes. Then a brown jackrabbit head bobbed up over the brush line. It was gone in an instant. She had not seen a rabbit in this area in a very long time. Was it a sign? She hoped it brought good tidings like it was supposed to. Inez had always loved rabbits. She always told Chonnie that it was her spirit animal. She would often dream of a rabbit that would lead her out of a dark hole. But it wasn't like that British Blonde girl's rabbit from that story. It was a brown rabbit, which she named Café Tsisdu. She used the Cherokee word for rabbit because she thought *conejo* was too ugly sounding. Inez smiled.

"Señora Plata, señora Plata. You must come quick. It's Ernesto," Alicia Garcia shouted when she exited the carriage. Alicia was Ernesto's wife. She was ten years younger than Ernesto. Married at the age of fourteen. Ernesto and Alicia had three children by the time she was seventeen, and now she was pregnant with their sixth child. So, Inez's concern wasn't only for Ernesto but for Alicia's condition.

"What's the matter?" Inez yelled after Alicia as she followed her into the servant's quarters.

"Ernesto was attacked on the road to Brownsville," Alicia said almost crying.

"Is he?"

"No, patrona, he is okay. But he wants to see you."

Confused, Inez picked up her pace and rushed in to Ernesto and Alicia's small house. She entered to see Dr. Yáñez checking him over. Dr. Yáñez turned to Inez and said, "He took a good beating but there is nothing broken. No permanent damage. He will be okay. He just needs to rest."

Relieved Inez said, "Thank you, Doctor."

Ernesto was laying on the bed with a bandage around his

head and another around his stomach. "Señora, it was El Rinche." Ernesto could barely speak because of a swollen lip, but he managed to get those words out.

"A rinche did this?" Inez could feel her blood pressure rising with anger.

"No, El Rinche. He saved me," Ernesto said through gritting teeth.

"What rinche?" Inez was confused. She thought he was still delirious from the beating.

"No, señora, it's El Rinche," Alicia stepped in to explain, "*Es un rinche fantasma*. He has been helping us. Pregúntale a mi suegra. She has seen him." Ernesto was Gloria and Nestor's youngest son. Inez knew that they had some trouble on the road a few months ago. They never said what happened though.

"Are you saying that someone dressed as a ranger helped you?" Inez asked, trying to understand what they were trying to tell her.

"No, señora, he said he was the ghost of all of their sins, and is back for a reckoning. He comes from nowhere. He has machetes and these strange stars he throws at people. One second he's here, and the next he's gone. His face is dark like a shadow, but he wears a rinche badge," Ernesto couldn't help telling his story.

"And he calls himself 'El Rinche'?" Inez said, sounding skeptical.

"No, he doesn't call himself anything. That is what mamá calls him. He stopped two rinches from killing us on the road. It was the day that we found the Saurez's. That was the day he came from the ground. Mamá said it was because when something real bad happens, God sends an angel to make things right."

"Okay, Ernesto, get some rest. I think they hit you pretty hard," Inez said dismissively.

"No, señora, I'm not confused. He said he had a message for you," Ernesto said, as she was turning to leave.

Inez stopped and waited for Ernesto to tell her the message.

Ernesto swallowed hard and said, "He said, *Can you hear the wind whispering and the crickets singing?*"

Inez felt the world spin as she finished his thought with, "…follow Café Tsisdu."

"What does it mean?" Alicia asked.

"It means, I have to go," Inez said, as she rushed out of the room.

She ran as fast as she could to the front gate. She didn't even wait for Orlando Serna, the guard at the gate, to open it for her. She unlocked the gate herself and pushed it open just enough for her to squeeze through. Inez ignored the yells from behind her to wait. She rushed to where she had seen the brown rabbit. But there was nothing there. The rabbit was gone. She looked all around. There was nothing. Saddened, she stepped backward. Crunch! She stepped on something. She lifted her foot and saw a single bullet. She picked it up and examined it. It was a silver bullet—shiny and new. It had two words etched into the casing:

Strong Enough.

UP THE WOLVES

There's gonna be a reckoning when the wolves come home.

"What the hell does that mean?" Pablo Honey asked his two Rangers tied to a mesquite tree on the road to Brownsville.

"I don't know. He didn't stop to explain. He just tied us up and left us here with this note," Jack Swann said, sounding very annoyed that Pablo had not untied them yet.

"Lt. Honey, can you untie us please?" Sam Hunt, the other Ranger, pleaded.

Pablo looked from one to the other and said, "Tommy, cut 'em loose."

Blind Tommy dismounted his horse, pulled his knife from his belt and proceeded to cut them loose.

"Now, tell me what happened again. This time don't leave anything out," Pablo demanded.

"We was heading down to Brownsville to get our whistles wet, when we spotted these two vaqueros. We thought we'd just rough them up a bit like we were supposed to, but then this thing came out of nowhere and took us both down..." Jack explained.

"What was this thing?" Pablo interrupted.

"The locals call it El Rinche fantasma. He's said to be the ghost of a Ranger that's come back to get us,"

"A ghost? Really? Ghosts don't write cryptic messages. This is a man. What did he look like?"

"He was dressed like...like one of us...he had a badge and everything...but he had a mask, two katanas and shuriken," Jack continued.

"What the hell are katanas and shuriken?" Pablo asked sounding annoyed.

"Katanas are Japanese samurai swords and shuriken are throwing stars. They come from the ninja tradition," Sam jumped in and explained.

"What the hell is a ninja?"

"A ninja is a mystical assassin."

"How the hell do you know that?" Pablo was infuriated at this point.

"We read. I became very interested in Japanese culture when I was living in California. Did you know they worship their emperor like he's a god?"

Pablo looked at both of them as they got to their feet and said, "I don't care. So, are you saying we got some sort of Japanese vigilante here?"

"No," Jack said, "He was a white man. Green eyes and Texas twang in his voice."

"Can you tell me anything that can help us find him?"

"No, but..."

"But what? Speak, goddamnit!," Pablo couldn't take it anymore.

"He didn't make any noise. He was quiet like a ghost. It looked like he didn't even have feet."

"No feet? What the hell is this thing?"

"Boss," Blind Tommy cut in to their conversation, "we've got to up the wolves. This ghost, or whatever it is, is taking out all our best guys. I mean, the reason we got Jack and Sam is because the wolves we want say the money ain't worth it."

Pablo looked back at the note and asked, "What did you say, Tommy? About upping the wolves?"

"It's just an expression, Boss. It means we need to get more bad gunslingers to help with this situation. That means more money."

"Upping the wolves, huh?"

"Yes, boss."

"Then we've got to go see the head wolf then."

James Stillwell was busy buying the Sierra rancho for $15 an acre from Pedro Sierra, when Honey and his men rode up to his office. Pedro Sierra was one of the last rancheros besides Inez Plata on the railroad line that had yet to sell. Stillwell gave him cold hard cash in a thick envelope and notarized the contract himself.

"It's a pleasure doing business with you Pedro," Stillwell said with a smile. He enjoyed this way of getting things done, as opposed to the violent tactics of Honey and his men.

Honey strode the front door with three men. One, he recognized as Blind Tommy, but the other two, he didn't know. Pedro got up and strode out of the office, shooting Honey and his men a stare filled with daggers.

"Jesus, Jim, another satisfied customer, huh?" Pablo said, plopping himself down in his usual chair.

"Well, you know, these are tough times with all these bandidos and such," Stillwell said, almost laughing.

"That's why we are here. We got a problem," Pablo said, pulling a cigarette from his pocket and sticking it in his mouth. Blind Tommy came up from behind Pablo and flicked on the Plata lighter. The cigarette's end ignited, and Pablo inhaled.

"It's this Rinche character, isn't it?" Stillwell's demeanor changed from amused to concerned.

"They say he's some sort of ghost," Pablo added.

"Is he Mexican?" Stillwell asked.

"Nope," Honey said, taking a long drag of his cigarette, "That's the strange thing. As these boys tell it, he's a white man or the ghost of a white man. Something like that."

"He's no ghost. I think he was sent from Austin."

"What? Why?"

"Apparently, they have caught wind of some nefarious activities by our rangers down here, and there has been word of a special ranger being sent to investigate."

"Bass Reeves," Pablo spat the words out with disgust.

"Who's Bass Reeves?"

"He's that federal marshal that's after me. He was there at that bumbled train fiasco. He must have said something to the governor. I should have killed him when I had the chance."

"Well, now. This ghost ranger might be a bigger problem than that, because the locals have been getting emboldened by his actions. They are starting to pull out of negotiations to sell their lands. We have to stop him, quietly. Because if he is sent from Austin then…"

"I hear you—loud and clear. Discreet but final."

"Yes, exactly."

"For *that* then, we are going to need more green to get the right kind of men."

"How much are we talking?"

"Enough for one special wolf—a shadow wolf."

HAIL MARY

Come with me, Hail Mary. Run quick, see. What do we have here. Now, do you wanna ride or die? lalala lalaladada. Bass sang under his breath as he bowed his head and loaded his .45's. One in the shoulder holster, one hanging on his hip, and one in the small of his back. This was his ritual before every risky arrest he ever made. Today was no different. They were here to take down the Shadow Wolf. The most feared assassin he had ever caught wind of. The Shadow Wolf started off as only whispers—rumors on the trail. Like Kyser Soze, he only seemed to exist in folklore—until he came for you, they would say. But as time went on, and the bodies began to pile up, his signature became clear to Bass. Two thin pointed daggers through the heart and one through the left eye. Always the left eye. No one ever saw him. So, when the warrant was written for his arrest. It didn't have a Christian name, but simply the Shadow Wolf. They say he got that name because he hunted from the shadows. He only stepped out long enough to kill you, then he was gone. How had they gotten here? Bass wondered. How had *he* gotten here?

A year ago, he first came down looking for Tal'dos. When he started the hunt for Pablo Honey, he never thought he would be squarin' off with the West's most dangerous boogeymen. What Chonnie had started here was something more than vengeance. For that, he was grateful. This new operation was about helping people. No killing involved. This was about justice. Even if the law wasn't behind it. It was still justice. When Bass was younger he would definitely have condoned this kind of operation, but now, things were different. Ever since Jim Crow started and he was forced to stand in the back of the room for meetings. Ever since he had to order from the back of restaurants and bring his own pail. Ever since they tried to frame him for murder. Ever since black and brown folks were getting strung up for being on the wrong shade of white. He felt the law wasn't always right.

We've been travelin' on this weary road—long time, till I take off this load. But we ride, ride it like a bullet. Hail Mary, Hail Mary. We won't worry, everything will come real. Bass continued to sing low and almost whistle. It was a habit he had picked up in his early years. The singing helped calm his nerves.

Bass breathed deep like Hiro had taught him, but that never really worked for him. He was too old of a dog to change his ways. But it worked for Tal'dos and Chonnie—the breathing. Tal'dos still had a heart filled with vengeance. Bass knew that the first chance he got. Tal'dos would kill Pablo Honey. It was something that Bass was trying desperately to prevent. Not because he cared for Pablo's life, but for Tal'dos' soul. Bass knew that murder never fills the cracks of a broken soul. It only deepens the wounds. But he couldn't say anything to Tal'dos—not now. Tal'dos couldn't hear him. So, on that day, six months ago, when Chonnie became witness to real horror and started to talk about doing things different, Bass had hope that this new path would soften Tal'dos' hardened heart.

It was a brisk Sunday morning and the moon had not quite let go of the sky. Even as the sun rose, it held on for Chonnie to slip out of the village and take the road to Inez and his true destiny. Some would call it an eclipse, but the moon knew that it was that rare moment when it got the chance to kiss its long-lost lover, the sun. And when that happens, new creatures are born. And in this case, it was new conviction that sprung from deep within the earth. Chonnie didn't travel to the Plata rancho on that day. He returned to Kondo Village—to Tal'dos, to Bass, to Hiro, and to his training, like a man possessed with conviction.

"What happened to you out there?" Tal'dos was the first to see Chonnie as he returned.

Chonnie wore the face of guilt, of devastation—but also the seeds of righteousness. "They killed 'em all. Violated them, and hung them from a…"

"Who? Who's dead?" Tal'dos felt his heart jump into his throat.

"The Saurez's. They were good people. They worked for my family for years. They didn't deserve this. We did this."

"What do you mean?"

"They nailed signs into the little girls. *You take 2 of ours. We take 4 of yours.*"

"They couldn't have known it was us. No way."

"We were just Mexicans to them. So, we kill two white boys…"

"…they kill four brown folks," Bass entered the conversation, striding back from his early morning walk with Hiro. "I've seen this before. In the Arkansas territory, every time a white got killed, they would send a message by killing two black folks. Didn't matter who? It's their way of teaching us a lesson."

"So, we hit them back harder," Tal'dos said, feeling his blood boiling.

"No," Chonnie said, "We need to do things different. It's not just Honey and his men who are doing this. Out there, there were two other rinches that were going to kill an older couple. Just 'cause they were Mexican. I took 'em out. But they didn't work for Honey. They worked for someone named Baker."

"Baker?" Bass asked, "Anthony Baker?"

"Who is he?" Tal'dos asked.

"He was the head Ranger Captain for this district. Now, I think he's sheriff of Hidalgo," Bass answered.

"Point is. It's not just Honey working for Stillwell. This goes deeper. This is systemic. It's the entire organization. They had orders to kill Mexicans. To scare Mexican Tejanos off their lands. Honey, he's just a thug for bigger villains."

"Honey is our target! We can't stop the entire Texas Ranger organization," Tal'dos said exploding.

"Maybe not. But at least we can mess with their operations here," Chonnie said.

"How do you propose we do that?" Tal'dos asked.

"From the shadows," Hiro answered, "Like ninja in the night."

"From the shadows," Chonnie repeated. "Like ghosts in the night. We can't take them head on. As bandidos, we would just get more people killed. But if they don't know what's coming for them. If we attack from the shadows. Create a monster for the rinches. Something they don't know is real or not. That's how we do it. And no killing. Killing just invites more death. We got to scare them into leaving on their own."

"And those green eyes and white skin of yours can help," Bass added.

At that moment El Rinche was born. An idea born from tragedy. Bred from pain, conviction, and justice. It was an idea so wild that it could only exist in *cuentos*, in folktales, in the shadows.

Now pay attention, rest in peace father. I'm a ghost in these killin' fields. Hail Mary, catch me if I go. Let's go deep inside the solitary mind of a madman who screams in the dark. Evil lurks, enemies see me flee. Activate my hate, let it break, to the flame, set a trap...

THE SHADOW OF THE SUN

What does it take to bring someone back from the dead? Does it take prayer? A voodoo ritual? *Brujeria*? For the Shadow Wolf, it only took a thousand dollars and a promise to kill the great Bass Reeves. There had only been two times in the Shadow Wolf's career that someone had gotten close to capturing the legendary assassin. And both times it was the same man—Bass Reeves. For the past ten years, the Shadow Wolf had disappeared in the tall tales of the American West. To some, the Shadow Wolf was just a story that outlaws would tell their kids. Rat on your pop, and the Shadow Wolf will come for you in the dead of the night, when the Shadows are at their darkest. It was a myth that persisted like *El Cucuy* or *La Llorona*. The truth though, was far from what anyone would ever believe.

The Shadow Wolf was flesh and blood. A deadly assassin that had chosen to retire and live a quiet life—until that letter arrived. It was sent in the old fashion. Addressed to Sheryl Baum. The letter was one simple sentence: *Who dances with the devil in the pale moon light? BASS REEVES $1,000.* The Shadow Wolf smiled.

Retirement had grown stale. Grandchildren now. If anything, this could be one last hurrah. Bass was an old man now. There was no way he was up for this fight. The Shadow Wolf turned the envelope over and saw the senders' name as Pablo Honey, and the return address as Brownsville, Texas.

Slim didn't know how he was supposed to get this message to Tal'dos. He sat at the Blue Laguna Bar on Adams St. drinking Mexican beer and carving away. This time he was carving a rabbit with long ears. He couldn't send the signal like he did every time he needed to speak to Tal'dos. Pablo Honey had closed ranks and didn't allow his Rangers to go anywhere alone. Rangers were getting roughed up regularly now. The attacks on the Mexicanos had essentially come to a standstill. Honey was furious and Slim was laughing on the inside. He had no idea that there was a rat in his crew. Honey was too hell bent on having *hombres malos* take care of the problem. To Honey, the problem was Bass Reeves and this ghost ranger. They just didn't know who or what this ghost ranger was. For all they knew, he was sent from Austin. That was a little fiction that Bass had spread through his contact in the governor's office. Honey and the rest of the Rangers were running scared, and that fear led Honey to contact a tall tale of a hitman—the Shadow Wolf. Slim had heard stories. This boogeyman would be an old man now, but Honey insisted he could get the job done. Legends don't age, and this legend was the worst of the worst.

This was information that Tal'dos would need. But Slim simply couldn't get away. Not with Sam Hunt hanging around him, talking all sorts of Oriental stories.

"Slim!" Honey called out to him from the back of the bar. Slim put his rabbit and whittling knife away and went to join Honey. Leaving Sam to babble to the drunks at the bar.

"Sam, watch the front door. Don't want this ghost ranger to slip in and kill us all," Slim teased Sam.

"Very funny Slim. You ain't never been at the business end of his shuriken. It hurt like nothing else," Sam said, cradling his bandaged hand.

"Just keep a look out," Slim said, as he followed Honey out to the alleyway. "What's going on, boss?"

"It's nearly midnight and still no sign of the Shadow Wolf," Honey said, sounding irked.

"Maybe the Shadow Wolf is just a story like they say, Pablo," Slim said skeptically.

"No, the Shadow Wolf's real. I've seen the handy work up close and personal."

"Yeah, fifteen years ago maybe, but he'd be an old man now," Slim responded.

"I'm like a fine wine, only gets better with age," a soft gravelly voice broke through the night, like only the shadow of the sun can do.

Honey turned to the darkened end of the alleyway, smiling while Slim gripped his sidearm on instinct. "Shadow Wolf," Honey said ecstatic.

"Pablo Honey," the soft gravelly voice got closer, "I haven't seen you in ages. Since you was just a little spitfire, running snatch-

and-grab jobs in Brazos County. My, how things have changed."

Just then, a dark figure stepped out of the shadows. And for the first time in years, human eyes laid witness to the Shadow Wolf. She wore a long, flowing, brown skirt with a black blouse. A broadbrimmed black hat with a mass of white and grey feathers stuffed into the brim, covering her long flowing jet-black hair. Her face did not show evidence of aging, like a woman in her late forties should. Her dark skin hid any evidence of wrinkles—just the crow's feet in the corner of her almond shaped eyes. The darkness hid everything else.

"The Shadow Wolf's a woman?" Slim was left dumb-founded.

"Sometimes," the Shadow Wolf said, "sometimes I am just a shadow. The last shadow men usually see."

"That's why Sheryl here is so effective. No one expects a woman," Pablo explained.

"But a *negra*," Slim said, shocked by even his own words.

"Yes, I'm a black woman. I was born in the shadow of the sun. You son, look like you was born in the light of the moon, *Paleface*," Sheryl was starting to get a little hot under the collar.

"Don't mind Slim. He's just…simple," Pablo said, trying to cool Sheryl down. "It's good to see you. Out of retirement and all."

"I ain't out of retirement, Pablo. I'm just here to kill Bass and collect my thousand."

"But wouldn't killing Bass Reeves bring down too much heat on us? I mean, he's a federal marshal after all," Slim asked.

"Not if the Shadow Wolf gets him. It would be an old

grudge being settled. No one would suspect a thing," Honey said, sounding pleased with his plan.

"What about the ghost ranger?" asked Slim.

"I don't care about any of that. I just want to kill Bass," Sheryl said, sounding very uninterested in the ghost problem.

"Patience Sheryl, this ghost uses the shadows like you."

Sheryl looked at him with a stare that, if Honey didn't know any better, had a glimmer of fear. "What do you mean? How does he use the shadows?"

"He seems to come out of nowhere. He uses these funny swords—katanas I think. And these sharp as hell stars he throws at people."

"Are you sure they are katana and not ninjato?" Sheryl's voice began to shake.

"Ninjato?" Honey corrected himself.

"Nevermind," Sheryl said, and then changed the subject, "And Bass is mixed up with this character?" Sheryl asked.

"I think so," Honey answered.

"Are there any Japanese settlements around?"

"Japanese? I think there's a chink woman that sells shrimp at the market square every day. If there was, she might know."

Slim swallowed hard. That was Itsuko. If they found Kondo, that would spell bad news for their operation. He had to get a message to Tal'dos. But how? He couldn't get away. Not without Honey becoming suspicious. He would have to do the secondary signal in the morning. It was his last chance to warn them. But he had to do it before they went to the market. He needed to stall.

"But I thought we were rounding up bad hombres. I've got Bad Billy Dang and Lester Bangs coming in from El Paso, and Jack Swann rounding up boys in Seguin. Reeves ain't the problem, this ghost ranger is," Slim said, trying to dissuade Honey from this course of action.

"We are, Slim. We are. But Reeves is the key. There's no better way to bring this lone ranger out into the open like the Shadow Wolf. They'll never see her coming."

SIMPLE TWIST OF FATE

It was a simple twist of fate. That is what they would say in the stories—in the *corridos*. But Tal'dos knew different. He had seen it. He just chose not to accept it. It was his burden from since he could remember. He had always been the Long-Eye. He could see over a quarter of a mile without the help of binoculars, but that wasn't all. Tal'dos could also see in the future in glimpses. Images that talked to him through the wind, through the stars, through his dreams, and he had seen this simple twist of fate happen. The moment Chonnie returned from bearing witness. He had finally emerged from the cocoon of his first death. He had become, and with that came conviction.

Chonnie took to his training like a man on fire. He quickly mastered shadow walking, the art of the ninjato. With Bass' help, he learned to perfect the art of strategy. Tal'dos, on the other hand, felt sidelined. He had been in charge of running this crew, and now Chonnie had become the leader. What was worse was that everyone instantly accepted his leadership and his plan. No question. No discussion. It just felt right to everyone. Tal'dos knew it was right. But they seemed to be forgetting why they were there in the first place. To kill Pablo Honey.

"Penny for your thoughts," it was Bass. He had found Tal'dos staring into the ocean as the sun set.

"I'm alright, Bass. You can go back to Chonnie," Tal'dos said, knowing that Bass was just checking up on him.

"Feeling like Little Teddy on the playground?"

"What? Who's Little Teddy?"

"Just a children's story. Little Teddy was always the smallest, slowest, and downright most insignificant kid on the playground. He was never picked for any of the games. He was just left to play in the dirt by himself. But you know what happened?"

"What happened?" Tal'dos asked reluctantly.

"He grew up. He became President. You see, Little Teddy had one thing the other boys didn't have. He had drive. He would never give up. Even when they told him he couldn't do something, he doubled down. And when he failed, which he did a lot, he found a new way to get things done."

"Bass, I'm not some little kid looking for a purpose in life. I saw this coming. I just…"

"…feel a little left out because this has become more than just a plan to kill Honey."

"Yeah."

"It happens. But you know that the road to justice isn't just covered in blood. It has to be built on service to something greater than your own pain. That's what's going on here, and you know it," Bass explained, sounding like the father he never had.

"Sometimes, Bass, you are more of a father than mine ever was," Tal'dos said, feeling his heart leak just a little bit.

"Running Coyote was a great partner. Always had my back. Great at tracking. But he never learned to love himself, not even a little. That is why he was never there for you or Mape'l."

"You always defend him, don't you Bass?"

"You only ever see the bad he did. There was good in him too."

"He never stuck around long enough for me to see that good you talk about."

"Tal'dos, come with me. I want to show you something," Bass said, waving Tal'dos back toward the village.

Tal'dos hesitated for a second and then reluctantly followed ol' Bass. Tal'dos watched as he struggled to step in the shifting sands of the beach. He was such an imposing figure when Tal'dos was a kid. He was bigger than any man Tal'dos had ever seen. Now, though, old age left him more feeble than Bass would ever admit. Tal'dos could see the arthritis bothering his hands in the morning. He could see the pain he had pissing. But Bass still had that stare that brought men to their knees.

"You know," Bass started talking as they approached his hackcart, "Your father knew when you were born that you had the Long-Eye. He was there when Mape'l pushed you out of her. He was the first to hold you. And as you cried, Running Coyote looked into your eyes and said, 'those are long eyes.'"

"My mother never told me that story."

"She never knew. It was something between me and Running Coyote."

"When you was four years old. He took you to go shooting for the first time. And you took down a deer, first shot. It was amazing."

"I remember that, but I don't remember him there. I just remember you."

"You don't want to remember him there, but he was. That was the first time I heard him call you Long-Eye."

Bass and Tal'dos reached the cart, and Bass felt under the bed of the cart for something. He fiddled around with a latch, and then Tal'dos heard a click. Bass reached under the cart with both hands and slid out a long wooden box. "Bass, you are full of surprises. I didn't know you had secret compartments on this thing."

"You can never be too careful. I always have an ace in the hole. But this here isn't for me. When Running Coyote died, he didn't want me to help you find Honey. He wanted me to give something to you. You see, your daddy had the long eye too, but it was nowhere near as strong as it is with you," Bass gestured for Tal'dos to help him open the tailgate of the cart. Tal'dos did so, and Bass put the long box on the tailgate. "When we were at our best, when my legend was at its height, people feared me because they thought I was protected by Cherokee magic. Never was shot. Not once. That is what the stories say, but it ain't true. I been shot. I just never let them see me bleed. But the man that helped me cook up the legend of Bass Reeeves was none other than your father. When I would walk into a bad showdown, like I had a pair of iron *huevos*, your daddy was the one that covered my ass. He was my protective spirit. No one would ever see him. He perched himself up and high, and with this he created my legend," Bass said, as he opened the box to reveal a .50 calibre Sharps rifle.

"Is that a Sharps rifle? I've never seen one of those up close. They say this is the deadliest long-range rifle," Tal'dos said with a bit of excitement.

"This was your daddy's weapon of choice. He said he got it from a rough-and-tumble buckaroo that said he could shoot 900 yards. Even went to Australia to prove it. But this rough-and-tumble buckaroo had an affinity for the Indian peoples. The job they wanted him to do was to kill Australian Injuns. He had none of that, and so he came back with a new woman and a new lease on life. Gave up the gun in a shooting contest which your daddy won. He used that gun for the rest of his days. On his deathbed, he told me that the gun belongs to the real Long-Eye. You."

Tal'dos looked at Bass and then back at the rifle and picked it up out of the box. It was lighter than he thought, but still carried a mighty heft. He put the gun in shooting position under his arm and flicked up the site. He lined up the site to settle on a can sitting on a post a hundred yards down the beach. "You got shells for this thing?"

"Of course," Bass said, pulling a box of bullets from the long box and handing them to Tal'dos. He popped open the rifle and loaded it. Tal'dos lined up the shot again, clicked the first trigger, then the second—firing the shot. It was so loud, it cracked the wind. The can exploded into too many pieces to count. Tal'dos smiled and said, "I will call her Duyukdu."

"Justice. Good name."

Bass touched Tal'dos' shoulder and said, "Chonnie needs you. You have a much better mind for strategy than that boy will ever have. Are you in?"

A shout from the village interrupted their conversation. It was Mayako, Itsuko's youngest daughter. She was shouting something in Japanese. They couldn't understand, but then Chonnie appeared. He was cradling his shoulder. Then he collapsed.

Tal'dos and Bass rushed to see Chonnie, still in ghost ranger costume, lying on the ground with a thin blade sticking out of his back. Bass recognized it right away. Chonnie was trying to speak but he seemed too out of breath.

"Take a deep breath, Chonnie. Tell us what happened," Bass said, trying to calm Chonnie.

"They took her."

"Took who?" Tal'dos asked.

"They took Itsuko," Chonnie answered.

"Who took her?" Hiro said, appearing out of nowhere.

"She said she was the Shadow Wolf," Chonnie said sounding deeply guilt ridden.

"No!" Bass said, feeling his mouth go dry.

"Who's the Shadow Wolf?" Tal'dos asked.

"Our worst nightmare," Bass said, sounding more frightened than anyone there would have liked.

THE WORST DAY SINCE YESTERDAY

Sometimes when Itsuko awoke in this new land, she could swear she was back in her bed in Japan. Then the humidity would seep in, and she remembered she was in a strange land. At least they were on the beach, she told herself every morning. That was one thing she didn't have back home. Being part of this Kondo fishing village was new for her. When her husband died in the uprising of Chichibu—massacred by the Tokyo police, by the military—they took on a group of farmers with antiquated rifles, old katana-wielding samurai, and frustrated revolutionaries. It was so bad that Itsuko had to flee with the colony heading to the United States. Along with her, she took her two daughters and her brother, Hiro, who also fought in that battle and was seriously injured.

Since that day, Hiro had retreated into a bottle of Saki and stayed there. Even when they found a young Indian child on the the road from Houston to South Texas. He took the child in and

151

taught him the art of ninjitsu. Not even that could bring Hiro out from under the power of the bottle. Itsuko, on the other hand, couldn't really mourn her lost husband, Roku. She had to be strong for her daughters—Mayako and Junko. They were only three and seven when they left Japan. Junko, her oldest, took it the hardest because she remembered her father the most. Mayako only had fleeting memories of a bearded man who would play with her in the gardens. But when they arrived to their final destination of South Padre Island, Texas, they took to the culture and languages of the region much better than Itsuko ever could.

Mayako spoke both Spanish and English with an American accent. Junko still retained her Japanese voice and spoke the language with her mother. Mayako only spoke to her in English or Spanish depending on her mood. Itsuko liked the Mexican people there, but the Anglos always treated them with disdain. Especially when they would sell at the market, which was what they were doing today. Itsuko had no training in fishing. Her family and husband had always been farmers. Fishing to her seemed too unpredictable. Somedays they caught plenty, others nothing. They were always at the whim of the ocean. Itsuko liked order. She liked routine. Plant the crops one season. Harvest them another. It worked like clockwork, but Itsuko had to choose a fishing colony to escape with. Their family was wanted by the Japanese government. So she had to keep a low profile—for her daughters.

"Mamá, the ferry is leaving. We have to go," Mayako shouted after her as she placed the last barrel on the back of their cart.

"Mayako, please don't call me mamá. Call me Okaasan.

152

We are Japanese. Not Mexican or Anglo," Itsuko snapped at her daughter for being too Mexicanized. She hated speaking English. Hiro had taken to it quite well, but she resisted as long as she could. But this was America, and so she finally started speaking English.

"Sorry Okassan, it won't happen again."

"Where's Junko?" Itsuko asked.

"She's not coming. Goro asked her to stay and help clean the *camarónes*. Come on, we have to go."

"Calm down child, you are always in so much of a hurry. We will make it," Itsuko said, climbing into the cab of her cart and pulling the reins for the mules to move.

"*Ay Dios*, let's not make this the worst day since yesterday," Mayako said, jumping in next to her mother.

"It's always the worst day since yesterday," Itsuko muttered under her breath.

Sheryl Baum was dressed in a beautiful, flowing, flower dress, with a bonnet that hid her signature thin knives and her long black locks. She had the rest of her weapons tucked into unsuspecting and easily accessible places. She hadn't worn her assassin's instruments in years, and she was getting goosebumps from the coldness of the blades. She never took guns. They were too loud, too clumsy. She preferred the precision of knives. Sheryl walked the market, perusing the local wares as she waited for the Japanese woman to set up her booth. There were several Mexican pots, Día de los muertos figurines, and of course, all the fresh foods the region had to offer. I will come back when the job is done and pick some up for the grandkids, she thought. She hated referring to herself that way, but that is what she was. Too young to be, she had to constantly tell herself. She started in this business when she was sixteen. Released by her sensei and sent to kill for profit.

Her husband had no idea she was the Shadow Wolf. He still didn't. He was a nice blacksmith from deep Georgia that had moved to East Texas to make a better life. That is where she met him. They married when she was only seventeen. It was her cover. Her three children quickly followed. That was thirty years ago. Her children all had children now. She had been out of practice for too long, but in the last week, she had tested her skills. Seducing a local, bedding him, and then cutting him to pieces. It had been too long, but apparently her beauty still caught men's eyes. They always liked the mix of Negro and Japanese in her features. That was her deadliest weapon. Afterward, she felt alive again, and found herself walking the shadows with ease.

Slim was waiting too. He was watching the Shadow Wolf as she blended into the crowd. Slim also watched Itsuko and Mayako unload their goods and set up their shrimp to sell. No Junko though. Oh no, Slim panicked. Junko was the secondary contact. She was the only one that knew Hiro and Tal'dos' secret. Slim didn't know what to do. He needed to get a message out somehow. Then, like a miracle, he spotted the glint of binoculars off in the distance. They were definitely Chonnie's. That meant that Inez was there. He was always following her. Slim wove his way through the crowd, trying not to let the panic show on his face. He wove his way out of the market and up to the roof where Chonnie was perched.

"You know, rabbits don't usually hide on rooftops," Slim said, coming up behind Chonnie.

"You are still too loud. It's those boots. I heard you coming a mile away," Chonnie said, not surprised at all.

"You saw me?" Slim asked dumbfounded.

Chonnie got up from his prone position and turned to face Slim, "Slim, you don't exactly blend into a sea of brown faces."

"Whatever, we got a problem."

"Why didn't you go through the usual signals?"

"No time, and besides Junko isn't with them."

"Yeah, I saw that. What's going on?"

"Pablo has hired the Shadow Wolf."

"Who's the Shadow Wolf?"

"Ain't you ever heard of the deadliest assassin the West has ever seen?"

"Nope, I grew up on the rancho."

"Doesn't matter, she's here. She's after Bass."

"She?" Chonnie said sounding surprised.

"Yeah, Shadow Wolf's a woman, but she ain't no joke."

"Is that it? We can deal with that."

"No, the Shadow Wolf—she recognized your skills. Your shadow walking. She knows about the Japanese mumbo jumbo you do. She knows it's Japanese. She figured out that Bass is working with you. She's going after Itsuko today."

Chonnie, stunned by this news, turned his binoculars to Itsuko and Mayako. "Does she know who I am?"

155

"No, she's not after you. She wants Bass."

"Then she won't see me coming. Who is she?"

Slim stepped closer to the edge and pointed to a striking black woman with almond eyes near the citrus booth. "That's her."

"She won't attack until dark. She'll use the shadows to follow Itsuko back to Kondo. That's where I'll hit her."

"Are you gonna tell the others?"

"Not enough time to go and come back. I'll have to handle this one on my own."

"It seems like a worse day than yesterday, huh?" Slim said, wiping sweat from his brow.

"It always is."

BECAUSE THE NIGHT

The night is where shadows live. And the night sees nothing. It belongs to dark things—shadows. And shadows were made for hiding and running, not for fighting. That was the one rule for shadow walking. But Sheryl had learned a loophole. She could slip out of the shadows, attack, and then slip right back in. That was one skill she learned on her own and shared with no one. She never broke the one rule. On this simple reconnaissance mission, though. That would be challenged. Sheryl waited all day for the Japanese woman and her daughter to pack up their wares and head toward their cart. It would be dark enough on the road to the ferry to ask her a few questions.

"Sumimasen," Sheryl said to Itsuko catching her off guard.

"You speak Japanese?" Itsuko responded in Japanese.

"Only a little," Sheryl said in English, "I see you are Japanese. Are you heading back to the ferry?"

"Yes, we are," Itsuko said, suspicious of this dark woman with Japanese eyes.

"My name is Sheryl Baum. I wanted to know if I could

catch a ride with you to the ferry. The people I was with already left. I dillydallied too long in the Market. They seemed to have forgotten me."

"I've never seen you on the island," Itsuko said still holding her suspicion tight.

"I'm not from there. I am just visiting from back East. I have family there," Sheryl said, trying to win her trust, "My mother was Japanese, and she has relatives in Kondo."

"You don't look Japanese!" Mayako interjected. sounding deeply interested in this woman.

"I know. I am only half Japanese. My father was a soldier. He met my mother when she came through San Francisco," Sheryl lied.

"A black man like…"

Itsuko slapped Mayako's knee, quieting her daughter before she gave away too much information. Itsuko had learned several things from having a brother that was ninja. One was you never give away too much information. "Sorry, we don't know you…"

"Look, I completely understand. Strangers and candy and all that, right? I had to try though."

"Sorry, I am sure there is a taxi that could take you. Over there on Adams street there is a taxi stand. They will help."

"Thank you, but I am in quite a hurry. It's the last ferry and all. I'm a woman all alone and unescorted. It's getting dark soon. I don't want to be traveling alone…you know, because the night… and I can pay. I have $25 dollars," Sheryl did a masterful job pleading her case. She could be on the stage if she was ever inclined.

Itsuko weighed everything. A woman alone. She didn't look dangerous, and they did need the money. "Okay," Itsuko shook her head and gestured for her to step up the cab of their cart. Sheryl stepped up, and Mayako scooted closer to her mother. It was crowded in the cab, but it was manageable. Itsuko mushed her mules and they were off.

Chonnie watched from the shadows. He saw Sheryl con her way onto Itsuko's cart. This was going to be even trickier than he originally thought. Chonnie ran alongside them with enough distance so they couldn't see him. It was a good two hours before they reached the Port Isabel ferry. Chonnie knew he couldn't run that far, so he decided to stow away under their cart. He waited until they cleared the central part of the city. Then he leapt for the tailgate. He caught it with a slight bit of difficulty, but before he knew it, he was in the back of the cart—amongst the rotting shrimp and melting ice. From his vantage point, all he could see was their shoes, and that is when he saw that this woman, the Shadow Wolf, had jika-tabi shoes like him. She was ninja like Hiro.

The pain that coursed through his shoulder blade was worse than the bullets that Hiro first dug out of him. "She wore jika-tabi. Like the ones you gave me," Chonnie said as Hiro worked on him.

"And you escaped?" Bass asked sounding extremely concerned.

"No," Chonnie said reluctantly, "She let me go. She said I wasn't her contract. *You* are, Bass."

"How does she know Bass is here?" Tal'dos asked as Hiro pulled the thin blade out of Chonnie's back. Tal'dos covered the wound with a paste of Hiro's concoction.

Chonnie just bit down hard on his leather belt and screamed.

"It's the poison. That's why it hurts so much. I recognized it right away. This salve will counteract the poison," Hiro said.

When the pain had subsided a little, Chonnie answered, "Slim told me. He said that Honey hired this Shadow Wolf, and she figured it out because of my shadow walking."

"She is ninja. Trained by Fūma Kotarō. That is how she knew," Hiro said, wiping the blood from his hands and dropping the thin blade into a bowl of water.

"Fūma Kotarō?" Tal'dos said shocked, "That's *your* sensei."

"Yes." Hiro said, washing his hands.

"Where's my mother?" it was Junko. Her voice trembled with fear and anger.

Tal'dos turned to look at her. She stood in the doorway with Mayako at her side. Mayako was crying. "Junko, we are going to get her back."

"How could this happen? You were supposed to protect her," Junko said, leveling the accusation at Tal'dos.

"I know Junko, but...this was..."

"This is your fault. When I agreed to help you...you said nothing would happen to us," Junko was fuming now.

That is when Mayako jumped in, "It was my fault. I gave Chonnie away."

"It wasn't your fault. The fault was all mine," Chonnie said, pulling himself from the table. "We fought in the shadows," Chonnie said, looking at Tal'dos and then Hiro.

Chonnie never noticed how bumpy the road was until he rode in the back of this cart. He knew it was old and in need of repair, but still, it moved a whole hell of a lot. He rode and tried to listen to the three of them converse in the cab of the cart, but he could only make out talk about Japanese traditions and their fishing village. Then, the worst thing that could possibly happened occurred. The cart stopped. Mayako jumped into the back of the cart and spied Chonnie lying amongst the crates of shrimp and melting ice. Mayako had a big smile, and Chonnie just put his finger in front of his lips and silently mouthed, ssssshhhh.

But it was too late. Sheryl was standing right next to her. She had her daggers out and was about to fire one at Chonnie, but he leapt at her and pushed her into the shadows. She instinctively struck him in the gut with her knee and kicked him back. It was too late though. They were already in the shadows. She had broken the rule of shadow walking. The shadows seemed to see them now. It filled her with a dread she had never felt. Chonnie fired a shuriken that landed above her breast. She immediately fired her dagger at Chonnie. It hit him square under his right shoulder blade. They both fell out of the shadows and onto the hard ground below. They had torn a hole in the cover to their cart. Chonnie reached for his ninjato but it was too late. The Shadow Wolf had her blade at Chonnie's throat. It only cut superficially, but she held it there.

"I ain't after you. Not yet. My contract is for Bass Reeves. I know you're working with him. Tell him to meet me at the north shore—midnight. And I'm taking the woman for insurance," the Shadow Wolf said. As she quickly pulled her blade from his throat, she hit him square across the temple, knocking him out.

"I woke up in the back of the cart. Mayako was driving the mules, and here we are," Chonnie said, nursing his wound.

Bass checked his guns and said, "This is my fault. I will get Itsuko back."

"Will she hurt her? Will she hurt Kaasan?" Junko said, sounding almost hysterical.

"No," Hiro interjected, "She will not. Not until she has closed her contract. Then she will close all loose ends."

"I got to take care of this. I'm the one she wants, and it ain't because of some contract. We have unfinished business," Bass said, walking out of the room.

"We can't let him do this alone," Tal'dos pleaded to the group.

"I agree," Chonnie said, trying to stand. "We have to help Bass. This woman will kill him."

"Not you," Hiro said. "You are hurt, and you broke the only rule of shadow walking. I don't know what the consequences will be. No one has done that since…"

"Since what?" Chonnie asked.

"Since Hattori Hanzō. There is never anything good that comes from disturbing the shadows—nothing."

"I can't worry about that now. We have to get Itsuko back.

That is all that matters," Chonnie said.

"Yes, what do we do?" Junko jumped into the conversation sounding strong and steady.

"You can't go," Tal'dos said. "You are not trained. You will certainly get yourself killed."

"I won't sit here and do nothing. That is my mother out there."

"And Bass too," Tal'dos said, hugging Junko. "We will stop this Shadow Wolf. We will. But we need you here to watch Mayako and Chonnie."

"I'm going," Chonnie insisted.

"We only have three hours. Your wound will take at least a week to heal," Tal'dos said.

"I can still do this," Chonnie said, trying to deny the fact that he couldn't move his right arm.

"No," Hiro stepped up. "I will go. Itsuko is my sister. This Shadow Wolf is ninja. I will handle this."

"But you're not well enough for this either," Tal'dos said, sounding concerned.

"If this is my end, then so be it. This is Itsuko. I will not fail her," Hiro said, storming out of the room.

"Junko, Mayako, go with Hiro. Help him, please," said Tal'dos.

Junko and Mayako reluctantly followed their uncle.

"We can't kill her, you know that," Chonnie said to Tal'dos.

"I know. But we can't tell Junko that."

"She is the key to getting Honey once and for all. They

163

have gotten too close to finding out about us. We have to stop him now," Chonnie said.

"I know. But capturing a skilled ninja like the Shadow Wolf is going to be near impossible. Because the night is the shadow's home, and only ninja know how to play in the shadows. But she broke the rule. That is our advantage."

"What does that mean?—the rule of the shadows. Hiro never talks about it," Chonnie asked.

"It's never good. But I have seen this night. I just didn't know it was so soon. Bass is truly in trouble," Tal'dos responded.

"Do you think she expects Bass to come alone?" Chonnie asked, getting to his feet.

"No. She is ninja. But we have one advantage. She doesn't know about me and my rifle, Duyukdu."

JUST LIKE SUICIDE

The shadows are unrelentingly secret. They are worse than the freemasons. Nothing is really known about them, except that no light is allowed to pass through, and they abhor loud noises. Like dogs with fireworks, they hate it. That was their real problem with fighting within them. Not the physical act, but the sounds it makes disturbs their dark quiet existence. So, when Chonnie and Sheryl fought within the shadows, it caused so much discomfort that the shadows swore punishment to the offenders.

*Ready or not, here I come, you can't hide. Gonna find you and take it slowly. Ready or not, here I come, you can't hide. Gonna find you and make you...*Sheryl sang under her breath. She was still sore from the fight with the pathetic excuse of a ghost ranging American ninja. She didn't think he was going to be as unpredictable as he was. The ninjato, the jika-tabi. There was something familiar about the style. She couldn't quite place it.

*Everyone would have a gun in the ghetto of course, when giddyuping on their horse. I kick a rhyme drinking moonshine. I pour a sip on the concrete, for the deceased. But no don't weep...*the singing helped. It helped to steady her. It was something she had learned from Bass Reeves. But he didn't know it. She had watched him, back in the day. She respected him because he got close to seeing her. Not once but twice. He was the only one that she swore could see her through the shadows. But then came that night…

I play my enemies like a game of chess, where I rest. No stress, if you don't smoke sess. Lest—I must confess, my destiny's manifest…

Itsuko was bound like a witch tied to a stake. But instead of a stake, it was a marker post for rising sea levels. Her hands were bound around the post. So she didn't have much room to struggle. "Kuso!" she muttered to herself. This was all Hiro's fault. She knew that when he started training that Mexican white boy that there was going to be trouble. But his spirits were so lifted. He didn't drink as much as he used to. It was like he had purpose again. So, she let it go. It didn't affect any of her business or her life in the village. She thought that maybe one of *them* would get hurt—not her. She was scared to death because she didn't know what that ninja woman did with Mayako.

"Don't worry," Sheryl said, stepping from behind her. "This will all be over soon. Once Bass is dead, my contract is closed." She was no longer wearing her flower-printed dress, but full ninja uniform except that her face was uncovered.

"What about my daughter?" Itsuko pleaded with her.

"She's fine. I'm no monster. I sent her back with that sorry excuse for ninja."

Itsuko knew all too well about ninja contracts, and the one

thing that she knew best is that contracts are never closed unless all loose ends are tied, and Itsuko was a big loose end. "Why Bass? He's a good man. He's police. Isn't that against the code?"

"How do you know about the code?"

"I'm Japanese. I know about ninja."

"This is different. This is America. Those rules don't apply here. You know how many lawmen I killed in my day? Nobody cares."

Itsuko knew there was no such code, but she wanted to test how much this woman knew about ninja, and she had her answer. This woman was trained here. Itsuko thought Hiro and the others might have a chance.

Bass strode north down the beach. The moonlight to his right. It seemed to hang high tonight. Not much shine on the waves. He knew that facing the Shadow Wolf might be the last thing he did, but he had grown quite fond of Itsuko, and he was almost sure she was fond of him too. If he wasn't married, he would think of taking up courtship with her. She was a striking woman. Strong sharp features and soft disposition. *If saving her life is the last thing I do*, Bass thought, *it ain't such a bad end to ol' Bass Reeves.*

He saw the fire in the distance. The hairs on the back of his neck stood up. "This is just like suicide," he muttered under his breath. "What am I thinking, coming alone? This is a trap, for sure." Bass pushed through his fear and headed straight into the trap. He saw Itsuko just over a sand dune, five feet from the fire. No sign of the Shadow Wolf. Bass swallowed hard and strode into the range of the firelight.

"I'm here," he shouted into the night, "Let's do this."

Nothing. Just the sound of waves crashing. Then a report from a rifle. And out of the corner of his eye, a shadow moved. Bass reached for his .45 Long Colt and pointed it in the direction of the shadow. A bang made the sand shoot up, and a body came barreling down. It was dressed all in black. Hair in a bun on top her head. She screamed cradling her ankle. A knife fell from her hand. Bass stepped on her other hand, squeezing the other from it. Then he looked at her face.

"Sheryl? Is that you?"

"Hello Bass. Long time," Sheryl said as she slipped from under his boot and kicked him across the face, knocking him back a few steps. "We got some unfinished business, wouldn't you say?" Sheryl had two more blades in her hand. She leapt and was about to plunge the blades through both his eye sockets when she felt a hit across the stomach, knocking the breath from her. She crashed to the ground, and over her stood Hiro, with a jo staff. He said, "Well, that was anticlimactic." Then hit her across the back of the head, knocking her unconscious.

In the shadows, only the dark can see. That is an old proverb that never quite made it out of the shadow world. This is especially true of this night. The night that the great Shadow Wolf lost her privilege of walking amongst them. The shadows, always crueller than just, decided not to let her know she wasn't walking in the shadows that night. She only thought she was. That is why she lost that night. The other offender, though—they hadn't decided what to do about him. Not yet.

The throbbing took on a slow rhythm. It started slowing and then became louder. Thump, thump, thump. She tried to open her eyes, but they weighed like concrete. She struggled and opened her lids just a crack. The light invaded with a piercing pain that made the throbbing grow stronger, like someone was ringing her head from the inside. Slowly her eyes adjusted, and the pain began to lessen. The other pain from her foot became more apparent. She had been shot in the foot. She tried to sit up, but her hands were stopped by restraints. She saw cuffs locking her down to the bed she was on.

"I'm glad you're awake," said a soft Japanese man's voice.

She turned to see an old Japanese man with long white hair, a thin white mustache and goatee. He wore long, flowing, black robes. She recognized them right away, "You are ninja? Aren't you?"

"I *was*—a long time ago. There are no ninja. Not anymore. There are just old fools like me. My name is Hiro Akiyama. I was trained by the Shinobi ninja master, Fūma Kotarō," Hiro responded.

Sheryl struggled against her restraints. She felt a fear she had not felt since she was a little girl. Fūma Kotarō was the most feared ninja master of all time. He was her master too, and that is why she knew there was no way she was going to live past this day. Sheryl felt like she was surely going to die. "Why am I still alive? Shouldn't you have killed me by now?"

169

"I am not ninja anymore—remember."

"Then what do you want with me?"

"Do you know why your shadow walking failed the other night?" Hiro asked pouring two cups of Saki.

"What? My shadow walking didn't fail. I just…I just…" Sheryl said confused.

"Oh yes, it failed. That is how we saw you. Otherwise, that fight would have gone completely different," Hiro said, offering her a cup of Saki.

Sheryl looked at the cup and then back at Hiro. She nodded her head, and he slowly tipped the cup's rim between her lips. She drank. It burned going down and she instinctively coughed. "What is that?"

"Saki," Hiro said, "Or what passes for Saki here." Hiro downed his cup in one drink.

"It's terrible."

"It's an acquired taste. Fūma used to hate Saki. Did you know that?"

"No, I didn't. They say he was five hundred years old."

"Possibly. I never asked. But Fūma was many things. One thing he had in common with you is that he also fought in the shadows. Once—it was the night he killed Hattaroi Hanzō. He knew the rule. We all did. But he knew he couldn't beat Hanzō in a fair fight. Hanzō was too good. So, he chose to take the risk, and he pulled Hattaroi Hanzō into the shadows and finished him. That part never made it into the stories. It was a secret he only told his students as a warning to never fight in the shadows. He said it was just like seppuku, without the honor."

"But he survived. I survived. Nothing happened," Sheryl interrupted him.

"Except there was a price. He could never walk in the shadows again. He was banned for life," Hiro finished.

"But he continued to be ninja. He came here. He taught me," Sharyl said, irritated.

"Ahhh, that is what I was wondering. Fūma Kotarō never came to America. Whoever trained you was not Fūma Kotarō. He was an imposter. Fūma Kotarō never stepped back into the shadows. He resigned himself to teaching, and that he did until his dying day. I know, I was the last of his students."

"Your lying. I can't be banned. I can't," Sheryl said, hoping like hell he was lying, but deep down she knew. She had felt it that night, but she simply ignored it.

"I do not lie. It is the truth, and you know it," said Hiro.

"Then you're little budoka is banned too. He fought with me. Actually, he pushed me into the shadows," Sheryl said, fighting back in the only way she could.

"I thought so to, but he tested it, and he is still able to shadow walk. Maybe they haven't decided what to do just yet, or maybe they got the justice they wanted."

"Go to hell, old man! I'm not finished with you and Bass, or your little budoka. Not by a long shot."

"Relax, Sheryl. You ain't going nowhere," it was Bass. He came from the door behind Hiro.

"Bass, you son of a..."

"Sheryl, I got you. You going away for a long time," Bass said, offering her a cup of water.

"Is that Saki? 'cuz I could really use something a little more whiskey."

"It's water. Drink," Bass said, tipping the cup into her lips. She drank.

"I suppose you think you won. But I'm not done. I'll beat this."

"Sheryl, your foot is shot. There ain't no coming back from that. Not fully. That was a .50 calibre round that got you. You lucky you still got a foot."

Sheryl tried to wiggle her toes on her shot right foot, and she couldn't. What was worse was that there was no pain—none. That meant something far worse than death for a ninja. She panicked internally, but she wouldn't let it show. "What do you want, Bass? If you was really taking me in, I'd be shackled in a jail cell. Not in this fish gutting room."

"We want the man who hired you, Pablo Honey."

"I ain't never sold out my clients. Not once."

"This time is different. You ain't never been caught before."

"Still, I got my honor."

"You have no honor. When you take an innocent woman because you couldn't get to your target. That is not honor. That is cowardice!" Hiro burst out with an anger he didn't know he had.

"Still, I ain't tellin' you nothin'."

"Sheryl," Bass said, sitting on the edge of her bed. "I know what happened between us all those years ago was bad business.

Mostly on my part."

"It was all on your part. You just left me there. I was ready to…to give up the life."

"I didn't know who you were. What you were," Bass said softly.

"That didn't matter. Who I was then was still me."

"You are an assassin. I'm a lawman. We never could have mixed."

"That's what I liked about you, Bass. You was always standin' up. But not that night, huh?"

"It was a mistake. That I regret to this day."

"Really, well, you don't know the half of it."

"Sheryl, I have a deal for you." Bass changed the direction of the conversation.

"A deal, huh? What kind of deal?"

"You tell us how to get to Pablo Honey and his operation, and we let you go."

Sheryl laughed. "You can't be that stupid Bass. *I* sure ain't. You let me go. I finish you, or you finish me. That's the only way this ends."

"What about Silus? and Gregory and Tatia? and all them kids you got waiting for you back home? What happens when they find out who you really are?"

Sheryl relaxed. She fell back into her bed. She had never considered that. That life had always been separate. "You wouldn't do that?"

"You're the infamous Shadow Wolf. We send that story to

the papers and it goes everywhere. But if you stay retired, we keep quiet and you get to live your life with your family."

"You're a bastard, Bass Reeves. You always were," Sheryl spat with vitriol.

"It's a good deal, Sheryl."

"That's just like suicide to me, Bass. Even when I retired the first time, I still held to the idea that I could still come back."

"We old now, Sheryl. It's over for both of us. We got to leave the fighting and scheming to the youngins," Bass said, realizing that was meant for him too.

Sheryl thought about it and tried desperately to feel her toes, but she couldn't. If it was true, she was done. Then what was left for her, but her family. "Old? I ain't as old as you, old man," she said, relaxing her composure.

TALKING ABOUT
A REVOLUTION

There weren't many left. Not many at all to oppose the power of the Anglos coming into las *Villas del Norte*—what they would call the Rio Grande Valley. But a valley it was not. It was all a strategy to terraform this land from rancho to farmland. All they needed was Inez Plata's water rights and their plan would be complete. She had refused to sell and life on her rancho was getting harder by the day. Attacks on her cattle were more frequent. The sheriff was no help. He seemed helpless against the power of the King's and Stillwell. Inez could only get a dozen men to help with security. It simply wasn't enough, and Stillwell knew it. That was his plan. Everyone's spirit seemed broken. Then came El Rinche. This ghost ranger whose *corridos* were being sung amongst *la gente*. It was like they were talking about a revolution.

Inez walked the outskirts of her hacienda. She did this every morning. Ever since she found the silver bullet, she was hoping to see that rabbit again, but he hadn't returned. If it was the ghost of Chonnie, maybe his message had been delivered, and now the ball was in her court. She watched as the sun crept up the horizon and into the day sky. It was calming to her. She didn't have her Bennie. He hadn't been with her for months now, and that is how Inez wanted it. Safe in San Antonio with a bodyguard always keeping watch on him. It was a small comfort, but here on the rancho, she was alone. At night, she would often dream of Chonnie and not her husband. It gave her terrible angst because she loved her husband. She really did. But since their death. Chonnie was all she thought about.

Maybe it was because all the signs she had received since that day had been of Chonnie. Maybe it was unrequited love. She didn't know, but it gave her the only strength she had these days. She needed to fight Kleberg and the King's. She couldn't give up this land. Not after everything. But she didn't have the resources to continue this fight. She was on the losing side.

"Patrona!" someone yelled from the hacienda wall. "*Alguien viene!*"

Inez turned to look and saw a group of mounted men riding toward the hacienda. Inez felt for her pistol on her gun belt and quickly walked back to the front gate where her abuela's shotgun lay against the wall. She grabbed it, but she did not go in. Instead, two men came out with shotguns and stood on each side of her. She planted herself like a tree and waited. Shotgun locked and loaded. When they came close enough. She recognized Zefrino Puente riding up with a group of his thugs. Puente was the biggest *kineño* in

El Valle. He was the first to strike a deal with the King's, and many believed his men were the "bandidos" that had been terrorizing the other rancheros. She hated him for his snakelike nature. She hated him because when la gente would call him *Malinche*, Inez thought, he sullied the name of *Malinche*.

"Señora Plata. Buenos dias," Zefrino said as he came up to the front gate.

"Buenos dias, señor Puente," Inez said stern faced.

"It's a lovely morning. Wouldn't you say?" Zefrino said trying to break the ice.

"¿Qué quiere señor Puente?" Inez said coldly.

"Señora Plata. I've come to make one last plea for your sake. They are coming for you. I can't hold them off anymore."

"Oh, I didn't know you were protecting me, because I could have sworn I saw your vaqueros leading raids on my land," Inez said, holding her ground.

"Señora, I know what you may think of me, but I never wanted what happened to your *familia*. You have to know that. Herlinda and I took our first communion together. As boys, Daniel and I would often hunt together. Our families have always been friends. I don't know if you know our family history, but…"

"…don't lecture me on the history of *mi familia*. You think that I am not familiar with the history of this family?" Inez felt her blood start to boil.

"Apologies, señora. I meant no disrespect. I just wanted to let you know that I am still a friend, and to tell you that they are coming—los rinches. They are coming, and this time they won't come with contracts. They will kill all of you."

"How do you know?"

"You know how? They are coming in two days. I suggest you go to Stillwell and sell before they get here."

Inez looked at the men that Zefrino had brought with him. "And if I don't? Will you kill me?"

"No, señora, I have brought these men for your protection. Like I said, I don't want any more bloodshed."

"Thank you, Zefrino. But I will take my chances with my own men."

"Nonetheless, they have orders to stay here. Outside your front gates if need be," Zefrino said, as he began to turn his horse. "Good luck señora Plata. I hope you pray because you will need God on your side."

"I don't need God. I have El Rinche."

"I don't know if ghost stories can help you. Only God can," Zefrino starting to trot away.

"I don't know about that!" she shouted after him. "There's talk about a revolution. It starts here!"

Inez looked at the men that sat mounted in front of her. She turned to Miguel on her right, "Don't let them in. I don't trust them. But we can feed them." Inez then turned and walked inside the front gate. She was hoping they couldn't see her hands shaking. She didn't have the men to defend against los rinches and their *hombres malos*. She didn't know what to do. She reached for the necklace she had made of the bullet that Chonnie had left for her. It had replaced Zartan which she kept in the nightstand by her bed.

The bullet was easier to carry.

Inez then had an idea. She walked into the main house and into the kitchen. She looked around and found the meanest *chingona* in the room. "Señora Garcia?"

"Sí señora?" she said, cleaning her hands on her apron.

"You've met El Rinche before, haven't you?" Inez asked.

"Sí, he rescued us once, and he has rescued a few of the others," Señora Garcia answered, not sure where this was going.

"Do you know how to reach El Rinche?"

"I don't know. Maybe. *¿Por qué?*"

"We are going to need his help. Also, we need to get the burro out of storage. Just in case."

"Señora, what's going on?"

"They're coming for us. We need all the help we can get."

THE KILLING MOON

It was like déjà vu all over again for the stars and the moon. A year had tripped around the sun and here they were. Three men on their knees. Pablo Honey standing over them—smug and filled with bloodlust. Chonnie in the same position, but instead of Macario and his father to his left, it was Bass and Tal'dos. The stars glimmered deception again. Like a circuit finding a connection it had once lost, or a ship righting itself. It was a course correction, and this time, the killing moon was going to have its sacrifice.

Tal'dos rowed hard on the hidden boat that took them to and from the island. He had seen the end of this crusade for Pablo Honey. It was coming too soon, Tal'dos thought. Chonnie still wasn't healed completely. Things at Kondo were tense with the kidnapping of Itsuko. Junko was giving Tal'dos the cold shoulder now, when before they were close to something special. Mayako though, was goo-goo eyed over Chonnie now that she knew he was the ghost ranger. She spent plenty of time in the old fish-gutting station with them. It was obvious to everyone that she had a crush.

Chonnie didn't know how to let her know that his heart belonged to another. So, he did what anyone would do in that situation. He said nothing.

Itsuko, on the other hand, was furious with all of them. She had almost died for their stupid operation. Fighting the rinches, as she now referred to them, was futile. Like the farmers against the Japanese government. They would lose, and she wanted nothing to do with any of it anymore. But Bass—he was different. They often took long walks on the beach at night when the village slept. Her daughters were supposed to be asleep as well. But she often spied them watching her. Bass was a comfort she had not felt in a long time since her beloved Roku passed. Bass felt the same comfort. They both knew that the stars were not aligned for them, but in the moment, they didn't care. The nights were for them. And they took every advantage of the nights.

As soon as Tal'dos crashed the boat onto the shore, he sprinted off, dropping the oar and calling out to his crew.

Chonnie was the first to poke his head out of the fish-gutting station. "What's going on? What's wrong?" Chonnie said, sounding alarmed.

"Someone just ran a flag up for *el Rinche fantasma*," Tal'dos said, sounding irked.

"What does that mean?" Chonnie was confused.

"Somehow, those people you saved on the road all those months ago just sent out a call."

"What? How?"

Tal'dos pulled a rolled-up paper from inside his vest. It was one of our spies inside the Plata rancho."

"We have a spy inside my rancho? Since when?" Chonnie was a little upset.

"I don't tell you everything."

"Clearly. What does this mean?"

"They want to meet with El Rinche tonight at the abandoned hut where we found you."

"How do we know this isn't a trap?" Bass said, coming up on them with Hiro in tow.

"We don't," Tal'dos said, "But..."

"But what?" Bass asked.

"I saw the end. I saw it when I was handed this. They are gearing up for war there on the rancho. Zefrino Puente went by to warn Inez and left some men to help defend the hacienda. The winds of war are blowing now. It's a killing moon tonight. I think this is it."

"Have you checked with Slim?" Chonnie asked. "Is Honey making this move?"

"I just came from the dead drop. He verified that they will be coming for your girlfriend tomorrow night."

"She's not my girlfriend," Chonnie said annoyed.

"Right," Tal'dos said, while everyone else kind of shuffled around.

"She's not. She doesn't even know I'm alive."

"And it should stay that way. For everyone's sake," Tal'dos said sternly.

"What is that supposed to mean?"

"It means you are not coming tonight," Tal'dos set down his foot.

"What? But they want to see *me*," Chonnie was a little hurt.

"One ghost is just as good as another. Besides, she will probably be there, and if she even suspects you are alive..."

"Fine, but can I at least be overwatch?"

Tal'dos grunted and said, "Alright, but you don't come down. Not for anything."

"Alright," Chonnie said, kicking at the ground like a little boy that was just told he couldn't go out with his friends.

"I'm going with you," Bass said.

"Bass, we don't need you tonight. This is purely information gather. I'm going to see what they got to say," Tal'dos said, feeling something stir inside.

"Tonight's the killing moon. I feel it too. I need to be there. That's all I know."

Just then, Junko walked into the station. "Tal'dos, I need to speak with you," her voice seemed different. She had softened to Tal'dos.

"Of course," Tal'dos said, relieved she was speaking to him, "I will be right there."

Junko smiled at everyone in the room and walked just outside the door.

Tal'dos walked out of the room and said to the group, "Let's gear up. Sunset is within the hour."

"There are somethings in this world that are better if you let them sit for a while. Wine, tender hearts, and of course, vengeance," Pablo Honey said, as he stood over the masked ghost ranger, Bass Reeves, and a masked Indian. They all had their heads down like the ground was more interesting than looking at the man who was going to end them. "I know what you all are thinking. How could this happen? How could we be betrayed? Well, as a wise man once said, 'You can't trust the stars,' and you can't trust a turncoat either."

Chonnie raised his head and looked at Honey. To his right was Slim. He had a big grin on his face. "Oh," Slim said, sounding satisfied. "Did you really think I was going to turn on my own for a spic, a coon, and some Japs. Really? What kind of white man do you think I am?"

Directly behind Chonnie was Blind Tommy with his shotgun. To Tal'dos' right was Sam Hunt. But what worried Chonnie the most was that the Garcia's were trapped inside the decrepit old way station behind Honey. "Honey, your beef is with us. Let the Garcia's go."

"Oh, I plan to. But first they need to witness the death of this so-called Ghost Ranger. They need to sell that story high and wide. Break that rebellious spirit that those Mexicans seem to have because of you." Honey said, stepping down from the creaky old way station porch. He pulled a cigarette from his breast pocket and Daniel's lighter in clear sight of Chonnie.

"Where did you get that?"

"From a dead spic. Nice ain't it."

"Yes, it is. When all is done tonight. I think I'm gonna take that lighter for myself."

"Really? And how you gonna do that when you are dead?"

"You can't kill someone that's already dead. That's one of the benefits of being a ghost," Chonnie said, trying to get a rise out of Honey.

"Right, I already killed you. Didn't I?" Honey said, walking up to Chonnie and knocking his hat from his head, but left his mask secured to his face. "Who *are* you? I don't usually kill white men, but I'm gonna make an exception for you. It seems I already did, since you a ghost," Honey pulled his dragoon and put it to Chonnie's temple.

"I'm surprised Slim didn't tell you who I was. Seems like he told you everything else."

"He said he didn't know," Honey started to feel like something was wrong.

"Really? And you believed that? Seems like the stars aren't really to be trusted after all," Chonnie said with a smirk.

Honey smacked him across the face with side of his gun and turned to Slim, "Slim, what's he talking about?"

Slim shuffled a little and said, "He's just trying to save his skin a little longer. He's lying."

"It's a killing moon tonight, Honey." Chonnie said, feeling the blood seep into his mask. "But the question is, who's gonna do the killing, and who's doing the dying?"

Slim looked worried as Honey trained the gun on him. "You told me about the Indian here and you told me about Bass, but you never told me about the ranger. Why is that?"

"You know, you are such a white man," a soft voice came from Tal'dos' kneeling position. "Can't tell the difference between an Indian and a Japanese woman." The Indian figure picked her head up and removed her mask to reveal Junko.

Honey turned back and saw a young Japanese woman dressed in Tal'dos' clothing. But before he could clear his confusion, a bullet rang out, and the dragoon in his hand exploded. Chonnie sprung to his feet and knocked Blind Tommy's shotgun into his face. Smashing his nose and causing a geyser of blood to explode from his face. Chonnie then grabbed the shotgun from his hands and hit him across the temple, knocking him unconscious.

Slim shot the other two rangers and pointed his gun at Honey. Bass got to his feet slowly. He came up to Honey who was cradling a bloody and bullet-holed hand. "You under arrest now." Bass pushed a warrant into Honey's face and then punched him across the jaw, knocking him on his back.

From the ground Honey said, "You can't arrest me, and you know it. I'm still a duly sworn Texas Ranger. Your warrant don't mean squat."

"True, I can't arrest Pablo Honey, but I can arrest Timothy Mudd. The leader of the Mudd-Honey gang." Bass unraveled a wanted poster with Honey's likeness. But the caption read Timothy Mudd.

"That's not me. Mudd is dead. I know. I shot him myself."

"There ain't nobody to corroborate that claim." Bass shot back.

"Course not. I burned him…wait, no."

"It seems that Timothy Mudd has been masquerading as one Pablo Honey. That there is a serious offense. Impersonating a lawman."

"You can't do this. People know who I am. You can't," Honey pleaded with a smiling Bass.

"Shut up!" Tal'dos said, appearing from the brush. Duyukdu in his hands. "You're lucky you aint dead."

"Go to hell, Redskin! You think you won. You ain't won nothing," Pablo said, revealing the last card he had to play.

"What are you talking about?" Chonnie said, walking toward Honey.

"I knew this might not go my way. Slim playing a double agent. Come on. Slim ain't that good. I left a contingency in place. Just in case."

"What contingency?" Tal'dos said, leveling Duyukdu at Honey's head.

"It don't matter now. It's happening now. I told my men. The ones recruited under Slim's nose. They attack the Plata rancho tonight while I have you distracted," Honey laughed.

Tal'dos pulled the hammer back on Duyukdu but Junko put her hand on his shoulder. "Tal'dos don't…"

After a few seconds of considering his options, Tal'dos relaxed Duyukdu and set it down. Chonnie, on the other hand, smashed Honey upside his head in anger, knocking him out. Then he reached into Honey's pocket and took his father's lighter back.

Everyone looked at him. "What?" Chonnie said, slipping

the lighter into his own pocket.

"We have to get to the Plata rancho now. We are a good hour's ride though," Bass said.

"Then we have to ride hard, and hope they can hold 'em till we get there," Tal'dos said, and then turned to Junko, "Junko, you have to go back to the village. You have done enough today. Besides, if your mother knew you were out here with us, she would definitely kill all of us."

Slim walked down the porch area and said, "I will tie them up with Bass here. You guys go."

"Thank you, Slim. For everything."

Slim looked at Chonnie. "He killed my daddy. He's getting what he deserves. Besides, it felt good to be on the right side of things—for once." He then cuffed Honey's limp hands.

Chonnie looked up and saw the Garcia's staring at him. Without his hat, we was a little more recognizable. "Chonnie?" said señora Garcia.

"Junko, I know you are mad about what happened to your mother and I just want to apol..." Tal'dos said, trying to explain himself to the woman who made butterflies in his stomach.

Junko pressed her finger to his lips, "This isn't about that."

"Then what is this about?" Tal'dos said through her finger on his lips.

Junko moved her finger and then leaned in and kissed him dead on the lips. Tal'dos kissed her back hard. Tal'dos felt his heart skip a beat, and he took her in his arms. Junko pulled her lips away

189

and said, "I have something to tell you and I don't know how."

"What?"

"I received a message from that woman, Sheryl."

"What? Why would she send you a message?"

"She apologized for taking my mother. She said the moon tonight is not a killing moon. The stars—they deceive. And one other thing. But before I tell you, I want in on tonight's plan."

"It's too dangerous. If something happened to you. I wouldn't be able to forgive myself."

"I can take care of myself. Uncle Hiro has been teaching me aikido since I could walk. Besides, why do only the guys get to have all the fun."

Tal'dos grunted. "Okay, what's the message?"

"She said, don't trust Slim. He's not a friend."

Tal'dos walked back into the room with Chonnie, Bass, and Hiro. After hearing what Sheryl had told Junko, everything was clear now. He looked around the room and said, "There's a change of plan. Chonnie, you're back in. I was wrong. Tonight is no killing moon. It's a justice moon."

UNTIL WE FALL

Quisieron enterrarnos, pero se les olvido que somos semillas. *They tried to bury us. They didn't know we were seeds.* Inez found this proverb repeating in her head like a song she could never quite get out. It helped to distract her from the battle that was taking place outside the hacienda walls. Bullets were racing everywhere. The flashes exploding in the night sky like fireworks on *Dieciséis de Septembre.* They had come in the night like the diablos they were. Dressed like bandidos, but with white skin and Texas twang in their yells. Zefrino's men were trying to hold them off, but they were losing. Inez couldn't understand why they couldn't stop a few rinches. She figured there was something wrong here. Never trust a snake bearing gifts, or something like that. They kept on pleading for Inez to open the gate. but suspicion got the better of her and she told her men to keep it closed.

"Señora, por favor. They are too many. *Nos están matando!*" They were shouting at the gate. Inez hesitated. She still didn't trust them.

The bullets never stopped coming though. The assault had

been going on for about forty minutes now. There was no sign of El Rinche or the Garcias. Inez felt cold for the first time in this hot and humid night. She felt that this was going to be her last night on earth. She was going to fight. She closed her eyes and breathed deep. *And when I'm tired of feeling black.* She sung under her breath. *Spread the wings upon you're back. Take us high above it all. And stroke you're feathers till we fall. Until we fall, until we fall back down again.* She gripped the bullet around her neck.

Adán ran up to her. "Patrona! We have to let them in. They are getting slaughtered out there."

Inez opened her eyes and was about to speak when a voice cut through the air, "Who strokes you're feathers till you scream?"

Inez's heart skipped a beat and saw a tall figure step out of the shadows. He wore a large white hat, a black mask covering his mouth and nose. He wore a long overcoat, but underneath was a bandolier of strange metal stars and two ornate looking machetes. He wore a vest underneath that was made from what looked like black with white beads that created an image of a tree on his right breast. On the left was a rabbit with big ears. He had no boots though. It almost seemed like he had no feet in the darkness. But the eyes. Those *ojos verdes*, she recognized. Inez smiled wide and said, "Cho--"

El Rinche put his fingers to his lips and quietly mouthed, *shush.*

"You're El Rinche?" She quickly said instead.

"Give me five minutes. Hide everyone in the cellars."

"What are you going to do?"

"Open the gate."

"Ch—Rinche. Wait! I have the burro. He's ready."

"Where is he?"

"In the front foyer, locked and loaded," Inez said smilingly for the first time in ages.

Chonnie turned to disappear and said, "When I give you the signal. Let him loose."

"What's the signal?"

"Remember the COBRA assault?" Chonnie said, reaching out a clenched fist. She presented her open hand. He placed something in her hand and closed her fingers around it.

Inez looked down at her hand and smiled wide. She opened her hand. It was Zartan. It *was* Chonnie. She fought everything inside of her to reach out and hug him, but her men were watching. "Zartan will turn colors tonight." She looked back up, but he was gone. Disappeared into the night. Inez turned to Adán and said, "Do what he says. Get everyone into the cellars. Make sure burro is in position."

Joel Zacatecas and his band of men didn't know how long they were supposed to keep this charade up. Los rinches could only shoot so wide before Plata's men inside realized they were missing on purpose. Inez still didn't trust them, and for good reason. Joel had deception in his heart. He almost felt bad about tricking Inez Plata, but there was plenty of money to be had. And besides, he wanted to get Inez first. He had a thing for her. She was a beautiful woman, and those green eyes just drove him crazy. Zefrino had told them not to touch the women. But Inez was different. She was the leader. She was to be the example for the other Mexicanos. Resistance is futile. *Why not have his fun with her in the meantime?* he thought.

Vicente, his man closest to the gate, signaled to Joel. "The gate just unlocked."

Joel smiled and then fired three shots in the air. The rangers stopped shooting. The night was quiet for the first time this night. Eerily quiet with only the wind blowing betrayal, yet again. "*Abre la puerta,*" Joel told Vicente.

Vicente pushed the doors open and realized the courtyard was empty. Joel's seven men rushed into the courtyard. Guns drawn. Ready for a fight. But there was no one to be seen. Then the gate closed behind them and latched. This caused Joel to turn and look to see nothing. Vicente, on the other hand, saw something glimmering in the moonlight. It was sitting on the rim of the big fountain in the middle of the courtyard. Vicente walked up to it and saw it was a bullet standing straight up. "It's silver," Vicente said as he picked it up and examined it. Then Vicente's eyes went wide as he realized, "*¡Es El Rinche! ¡Está aquí!*"

Joel and his seven men took defensive stances, pointing their guns everywhere. But there was nothing.

Then a voice cut through the night, "They say this is the killing moon tonight."

Joel and his men looked around, but they couldn't see anything. The voice seemed to come from all around.

"That is why the stars are so bright tonight. But you can't

trust the stars. Not ever."

Joel afraid and angered by the voice said, "Come out and face us, or are you a coward?"

"Not a coward. Just buying some time."

"Time? For what?"

"For this."

The men all tensed up. Nothing happened. Then out of the shadows walked a tall masked man with a white hat that shone brightly in the night. "I usually don't like to kill. But tonight, you have given me no choice. It is a killing moon after all."

The men open fired in the direction of the masked man, but all they saw was a shattering of a mirror. Shuriken flew, catching three of the men in the hands, knocking their guns from their grips. Then the shine of blades as they tore through each man, cutting them in places that were not mortal, but severely debilitating. All but Joel. He stood alone at the end of the assault. His gun shaking from seeing something impossible. He was a ghost. He appeared and disappeared, and only the blades were visible. How was it possible? He *was* the rinche fantasma they had been talking about.

Joel blinked, and there was a blade at his throat. He could smell the blood dripping from it. Joel dropped his gun. "Are you gonna kill me?"

"Not yet. I need you to do something for me."

"What?"

"I need you to let them in."

Joel looked at the masked man. All he could see were those

piercing green eyes. Then Joel caught a shadow. It moved quickly. He could swear it was an Indian.

Bad Billy Dang and Lester Bangs held their seven men at bay after he saw Joel and his men go into the hacienda. After a few minutes, he saw Joel open the gate and wave them in. They rode toward the open gate, but when they got there, they saw something they couldn't quite fathom. It was a large brass cannon pointed right at them. It took a second, but Bad Billy realized that it was lit. And standing next to it was a small Mexican woman with green eyes. She covered her ears. Before they could do anything, el burro went off with a blast that shocked the wind. The cannonball land- ed in the middle of all his men, knocking several of them from their horses—killing a few of them instantly. Bad Billy and Lester had to hold their horse reigns tight when their horses buckled. Then they heard the report of a rifle and a shot exploded, grazing Lester's cheek. It was enough to open a major gash on his face and blow off half his ear.

Bad Billy looked at Lester, and the rest of his men were already running for the hills. He decided this was a lost cause and turned his horse. As he ran, he ordered the retreat.

"That's right! Run, you rinche bastards! This is our land. Quisieron enterrarnos, pero se les olvido que somos semillas. You tried to bury us, but you didn't know we were seeds!" Inez shouted after them.

Inez could hear the cheers from inside the hacienda and knew that they had won. She turned to see El Rinche and an Indian standing by the front door to the main house. Inez tried to run to them, but her workers began to crowd around her and hug her. They were shouting, "Viva la Patrona. Viva señora Plata."

None of the shouts were for El Rinche. They were for her. She couldn't hear them. She just wanted to reach Chonnie. But in the blink of an eye, they were gone.

WAKE ME WHEN SEPTEMBER ENDS

"Damn, I didn't know Blind Tommy weighed so much. Wake me when September ends," Slim complained as he and Bass loaded the last of the rangers into the back of the hackcart.

"What you talking about? This ain't September," Bass said, closing the gate and latching it locked.

"It's an expression my daddy always said. When things got bad or he had to do something he didn't want to do, he always said, 'Wake me when September ends.'" Slim said sweaty browed.
As Slim pushed the last inch of Blind Tommy's boot into the cart, he noticed some blood on his forehead. He removed his hat and wiped it clean.

"Tough getting blood out, isn't it?" Bass said stone cold.

Slim looked at him and said, "Yeah. It can be."

Bass turned his back to him and moved to mount the cab of the hackcart. Then he heard what he had been waiting for. It was the click of a hammer being pulled back. "I was wondering when you were going to make your move."

"When did you figure me out?"

"I didn't," Bass said, never turning around to look at him.

"Then how'd you know?"

"We didn't kill the Shadow Wolf like we said," Bass said, turning to face Slim's Long Colt pointing at his heart.

"What do you mean? Then what happened to her?"

"We don't tell you everything, Slim. Never can fully trust a turncoat and all. Just like Honey said," Bass replied, as he moved toward Slim.

Slim was feeling uncomfortable with Bass moving so close. "I don't want to kill you, Bass. But I will if I have to."

"You do what you got to, Slim."

"That thing you said about my daddy and Honey. Was that true or did you just lie to me to get me to work for you?"

"Oh, it was true. Honey's a cold-blooded bastard. But here's the thing. That don't change what you've done working with him. That's a dark heart. That's why I knew we couldn't really trust you."

"I did change. I did. I was with you all. Especially after what they did to that family. Those two little girls. But then Stillwell offered me more money to keep an eye on Honey. It seems nobody trusts anybody around here. That's when I realized, I could run this racket and get Honey at the same time. It was win win for me. But the end deal was to kill Tal'dos and Chonnie. That's the only way I could take over. You know how all that goes? But you, the great Bass Reeves. That's a tougher sell. Your death would just bring more heat. I can't have that. I was gonna spare you, Bass. I was, but now."

"Yeah, I know. But you remember the first time we met?"

"When Tal'dos coldcocked me? Yeah, I remember, why?"

"Well, you forgot what I told you then."

Slim's eyes went wide, but it was too late. A thin knife blade traced its way across his neck. Slim dropped his gun to grasp his neck. It was a feeble attempt to save his life, but it was too late. He fell back and just gurgled.

"I never travel alone. Especially when dealing with turn-coats," Bass said as he leaned over Slim dying. Behind Bass stood Sheryl. Her knife dripping with blood. "I'm sorry about this Slim. I really am. I ain't no murderer. I wanted to take you in, but you know our secret, and their mission ain't done. There will be more like you and Honey. And Tal'dos and Chonnie—they are needed. I couldn't have you exposing that. So I made a deal with the devil, and now we both going to hell."

Bass didn't know if Slim died before he finished or not, but he was dead for sure. So, he stood up, feeling a piece of his soul fall away. Then, Sheryl stuck one blade in Slim's eye. The other in his heart so they would know the Shadow Wolf was still there. Bass climbed into the cab of the cart with Sheryl at his side. She hooked her arm into Bass' and kissed him on the cheek. She leaned her head into the crook of his neck and said, "Where we going?"

"I got to deliver these boys to the train to Iron Heights, then wherever you want?" Bass said, sounding less and less like himself.

Sheryl smiled and said, "Let's go to Houston. We can have all sorts of fun there."

"Wake me when September ends," Bass said under his breath.

BORN AS GHOSTS

Tal'dos got the letter from a weeping Itsuko. Not Hiro like he would have thought. Bass was gone. He left without a goodbye. Just a note and a dead Slim. It was the work of the Shadow Wolf. That is what they would say. Her signature left at the scene of the crime to make sure the story stuck. But Tal'dos knew. He knew Bass did this. It was probably the only evil deed he did in his life, but like his letter said, the work they are doing—Tal'dos and Chonnie—is important. And Honey was just the beginning. They might have cemented themselves into legends. Born as ghosts. Songs were being sung all along the Rio Grande. Before, it was just El Rinche, the Ghost Ranger. But now there was the ghost of an Indian too. Who were these masked men? Tal'dos decided he wouldn't tell Chonnie what Bass had done. Chonnie saw him as a father, and he wouldn't understand. He didn't have the same darkness in him like Tal'dos. He didn't know about secrets, and lies, and the power they possess. Tal'dos knew all too well, and some day he would tell Chonnie, but not now. He was off to see Inez, and for the first time, Tal'dos felt like the winds were blowing justice. So, he crumbled up Bass' letter to Chonnie. He threw it into the ocean and walked away. The ocean, though, had other plans. It didn't like secrets.

Tal'dos walked back to Junko and Mayaki who were busy gutting fish to take to the market. He got to work with them while Itsuko loaded the cart. She hid her broken heart in a rose printed handkerchief Bass had given her on the night before he left. *At least*, Itsuko thought, *they had that one night together on the beach.* His scent was still thick on the handkerchief and on her.

Hiro sat in their converted headquarters (The old fish-gutting station). He started to fashion it into a good home base with weapons lining the walls. A proper table and some other items unpacked for the first time. It was Hiro's chest from his ninja days. They were going to need them. For the first time in years, his wounds didn't complain. He even started to drink only three cups of Saki a day, instead of seven. Eventually, he thought, he would give it up when he was dead. But for now, they were all born again as ghosts.

Inez walked around her childhood playground. The monte that her and Chonnie used to play in as kids. She wore her best green dress with the low-cut cleavage line. Her hair was down around her shoulders and she twisted the bullet in her fingers. She was waiting for her Café Tsisdu to meet her. It was a secret rendezvous, and it kept her up all night. But here she was at the break of dawn. Giddy as a school girl. Waiting on a long-lost love.

"Wow. You look amazing," Chonnie's voice caused a large

smile to form on her face.

Inez looked up to see Chonnie dressed in a brown suit with no tie. She couldn't help herself. She ran up and hugged him hard. So hard it knocked the breath from him. "I knew it. I knew it was you. Zartan. The rabbit. I knew it."

Chonnie pulled her face to his and kissed her hard. "I'm sorry—about everything. I shouldn't have left."

"It's okay. Your father needed you."

"No, I mean... I should have been here all those years ago. I shouldn't have left you."

Inez couldn't stop the tears from leaking out of the corner of her eyes. She kissed him hard again. "It's okay. You are back now. Everything will be better now."

Chonnie pulled away from her a little and looked at her like he had bad news.

"No, no no. You're not coming back?"

"I can't. I have to stay dead. Honey was only the beginning. There's going to be more, and these people—this place needs El Rinche. They don't need Ascensión Ruiz de Plata."

"But what about what I need. I can't do this alone."

"You have done it. You are stronger and better than I could ever be. They look up to you now. You got this. And I won't be far way. When you need me, just put a candle in your window. I will always come for you."

Inez wiped the tears from her face and said, "For how long? What about Bennie? What about your responsibilities as a Plata."

"I don't know. I just know that I have to do this now. I can't do this if people knew I was alive. They would just keep coming for you. This has to be our secret."

Inez knew he was right. The people had never seemed so determined to fight for themselves. Corridos were being sung every night to this Rinche—this ghost ranger. "Fine, but I have you for today, right?" Inez looked at him with eyes he hadn't seen since they were teenagers. It was a desire that stirred deep in both of them.

Chonnie smiled and stuttered, "Yeah."

Inez pushed him against their tree. He embraced her in a kiss so deep he felt it in his soul. Then they slid to the ground and embraced. Only the moon saw what they did that night. And for once, it looked away.

EL CORRIDO DEL RINCHE FANTASMA

by Juan Ochoa & Oscar Garza III

No hace mucho tiempo
No sé la hora ni la fecha
Fue cuando los mexicoamericanos balanceaban en el viento
Y los asesinos portaban una estrella.

Allá en el Rancho la Plata
Nació el Rinche fantasma
Y toda la gente canta el corrido
Del fantasma que peleó con los rinches y sólo él salió vivo

Todos menos la historia,
saben que los rinches son cobardes,
Matan por la espalda y sin misericordia
Para sus tierras robarles.

EL CORRIDO DEL RINCHE FANTASMA

Tengan presente señores lo que hoy les voy a cantar,
De un Rinche Chicano que los cobardes no han podido matar
De nombre Chonnie de apellido Plata.
Dejado por muerto pero se levantó como el Rinche Fantasma.

Un par de ojazos con la mirada fría,
Tan verdes como la envidia.
Piel blanca, pelo rubio,
Y el pecho lleno de rabia y de orgullo.

Mataron a su padre Daniel
Su hermano Macario también.
Los Rinches que son cobardes
Cometieron ofensas que son imperdonables.

Todos menos la historia,
saben que los rinches son cobardes,
Matan por la espalda y sin misericordia
Para sus tierras robarles.

Se los tragaron a balazos
El plomo cayó a cubetazos.
La sangre corrió por donde quiera.
Y todo por un puño de tierra.

Dado por muerto, Chonnie fue encontrado
Y curado con cuidado Chonnie sanó.

EL CORRIDO DEL RINCHE FANTASMA

Ya recuperado, en los artes marciales fue entrenado
Y se puso a buscar al que a su familia mató.

Quisiera poder arrancarme los ojos
Y no ver los cuerpos balaceando en el viento
Quisiera tener más que enojo
Quisiera dejar lo que siento.

Con sus artes marciales de Japón
Y con la ayuda de un cañón
El Rinche Fantasma enfrento en el Rancho la Plata
A los cobardes rinches quien atacaban a su amada.

Volaron estrellas, volaron balazos
Cayeron hombres hechos pedazos
No los quiso matar sólo los dejo heridos
A la cárcel mando a los traidores perdidos.

En la noche cuando escuchas un ruido
Acuérdate del Rinche Fantasma y cántale su corrido
Ya no tendrá que tener miedo ningún mexicoamericano
Vendrá el Rinche Fantasma con su katana en la mano.

THE CORRIDO OF THE GREEN-EYED MEXICAN

by Juan Ochoa & Oscar Garza III

He comes rolling in with the shadows,
Looking for the cowards who turned mesquites into gallows.
Ranger what can you do,
When the one you hunted comes after you?

If I could tell the story,
I would tell it well
About the cowardly rangers
And how I wished they'd go to hell.

Cowardly rangers lie awake in bed
Thinking of the man they left for dead.
After he was nursed back to health,
The Ghost Ranger was taught to fight with stealth.

But now deep in the night
The cowards lie praying for the light
Because somewhere in this land
Is a green-eyed Mexican with a katana in his hand.

If I could tell the story,
I would tell it well
About the cowardly rangers
And how I wished they'd go to hell.

They killed his father and his brother too
But they didn't see the job all the way through.
Pablo Honey you killed my family
And left my neighbors hanging from a tree.

I was trained by a ninja from Japan
And I'm going to stop your murdering clan.
Chonnie's coming and he's making a stand
Fighting from the shadows, katana in hand.

If I could tell the story,
I would tell it well
About the cowardly rangers
And how I wished they'd go to hell

Ranger what can you do?
The Ghost Ranger can strike anytime he wants to

With skills from the land of the rising sun
Chonnie comes ready for anyone.

Long ago but not so far away
When there was even more hate than today
The cowardly rangers hunted men for game
And bathed themselves in murdering fame.

If I could tell the story,
I would tell it well
About the cowardly rangers
And how I wished they'd go to hell.

But history is written by the winners
And makes heroes of sinners
For too long the rangers' tales have lied
But the truth isn't like the people who died.

The truth will live on the lips that whisper the stories
Of how cowards sought to bathe in glory
But ran like pigs from a knife
Anytime a Mexican defended his life

Ranger you may have stolen all the land
And you raped and murdered with a free hand
But you were always afraid and ran
When you saw a green eyed Mexican with a katana in his hand.

Christopher Carmona is the author of *The Road to Llorona Park*, which won the 2016 NACCS Tejas Best Fiction Award and was listed as one of the top 8 Latinx books in 2016 by NBC News. He was the inaugural writer-in-residence for the Langdon Review Writers Residency Program in 2015. He has three books of poetry: *140 Twitter Poems, I Have Always Been Here* and *beat.* He co-edited *The Beatest State In The Union: An Anthology of Beat Texas Writings* with Chuck Taylor and Rob Johnson and *Outrage: A Protest Anthology about Injustice in a Post 9/11 World* with Rossy Evelin Lima. He has also co-written *Nuev@s Voces Poeticas: A Dialogue about New Chican@ Poetics.* Currently, he is co-editing *Outrage: Witness and Silence* and is working on a series of bilingual YA novellas entitled *El Rinche: The Ghost Ranger of the Rio Grande.*

CPSIA information can be obtained
at www.ICGtesting.com
Printed in the USA
FSHW01n0820180818
51346FS